"A man could go mad with you in his arms!"

Julian pulled away, letting Merissa go with obvious reluctance. "You said I had to play a part," she whispered shakily in her defense. "I—I can act really well."

"That was no act!" he ground out roughly. "And if it was, then a very dangerous act with a very obvious ending. But I expect you know that, having so clearly been there before."

Merissa felt too shaken to protest. After all, what did it matter what he thought of her? "I know when to stop," she said in a brittle voice.

"I'm glad to hear it," Julian rasped, "because I've just discovered that I don't."

Merissa felt miserable, wondering what was happening to her. It was only a job, but her response to Julian had not been an act.

PATRICIA WILSON used to live in Yorkshire, England, but with her children all grown up, she decided to give up her teaching position there and accompany her husband on an extended trip to Spain. Their travels are providing her with plenty of inspiration for her romance writing.

Books by Patricia Wilson

PATRICIA WILSON

impossible bargain

Harlequin Books

TORONTO • NEW YORK • LONDON
AMSTERDAM • PARIS • SYDNEY • HAMBURG
STOCKHOLM • ATHENS • TOKYO • MILAN

Harlequin Presents first edition November 1988
ISBN 0-373-11125-8

Original hardcover edition published in 1987
by Mills & Boon Limited

CHAPTER ONE

'OH, HELL!' Hugh Goddard muttered, and Merissa raised amused eyes to his as he turned quickly to look in the other direction, his face just a little flushed as he caught her mocking glance.

'Is that just a general remark about the restaurant, or was there something particular that you had in mind?' she queried innocently.

For a second he looked just a little exasperated with her, his eyes running over her beautiful but mocking face. She had a skin like silk, sun-kissed and flawless, her eyes almond-shaped, almost oriental, dark, long-lashed and holding a mysterious attraction that came out so well in photographs. There was a sweetness to her face, to her softly curved lips, that even her practised mockery could sometimes not hide, and the clouds of light brown hair, naturally streaked with gold, that caught the lamplight in the crowded restaurant, framed a face that was heart-shaped and intriguing.

She held his gaze, her amusement growing, and he suddenly laughed, his tight expression relaxing as he reached across and captured her hand.

'You always get the better of me, Merissa Troy, do you know that? One of these days I'm going to get in under that guard. I remember when you weren't like this at all.'

'Are you going to explain the sudden oath or do I have to look around the room and guess?' Merissa asked wryly, making a great effort to keep the mocking smile on her face, to keep the hand beneath Hugh's relaxed. Being reminded that she had once been trusting and gentle had taken the gloss from the evening, and she knew she would have to fight hard to get back into the easygoing mood she had cultivated for these occasions.

'As a matter of fact,' he said quietly, 'I'm beginning to wish we were anywhere but here right now.' He lowered his voice and bent closer. 'I've just spotted two people that I could very well do without seeing. One's business, which I'm not at all interested in when I'm with you. The other is trouble.'

'Trouble?' She started to look round, but he pressed her hand and shook his head. 'Which one is trouble? What kind of trouble?'

'Never mind that one!' he said stiffly, still so obviously making an effort to calm down. 'He'll keep, the business won't. Jeff Clarke just came in and I could well do without him sauntering over here. Can you sit here alone for a minute while I have a word with him?' Hugh looked so agitated, so unlike his normally suave self, that Merissa forgot her cool, mocking shell for the moment. Somebody had really got under his skin just by being here. She nodded, smiling.

'Of course—I'm not a shy wallflower. Off you go and deal with the business end of things. I'll sit here and try to spot the trouble,' she smiled across at him, and his face darkened again.

'Don't attract anyone here, Merissa,' he warned with just the edge of anger in his voice. 'You attract enough attention as it is. I'm usually jealous when we're out. I shan't be more than a couple of minutes.'

He got up and walked across the crowded room, his back stiff with annoyance, and she watched him with speculation. He really was rattled! To see Hugh Goddard upset by anything or anyone was astonishing. In all the years she had known him he had never shown anything other than good humour and an ability to cope with anything that came along. Now he looked just a little—anxious, no, more than that; he was on the verge of being scared!

Merissa understood that feeling well enough and she recognised it in others instantly. She was usually scared herself, hence the mocking shell, the amused hardness that she had perfected. She had good reason to be constantly anxious, but Hugh was very different, a big success, polished and sophisticated. He had no reason to pretend.

She decided to take his advice and keep her eyes on the drink in her hand, swirling the martini round idly in the glass, watching the colour change in the light. Soon she would have hypnotised herself, she thought with a little smile, or spilled the whole thing down the front of her pale turquoise dress. The truth was that she was now suddenly afraid to look up.

She had had a strange feeling ever since they had come into the room a few minutes ago that she was being watched—not that she was unused to that, her job made her the focus of many eyes, more often than not, and she was quite hardened to it now. This was different, though. She felt that someone was compelling her to look round, to home in on the eyes she was sure were watching her, and now that Hugh had gone the feeling was overpowering, as if the watcher now had free rein to concentrate on her alone and order her eyes to rise.

For a few more seconds she resisted and then the unseen watcher won. She lifted her gaze slowly and warily, knowing by some odd instinct where to look. Of course she tried to be unaffected, indifferent, pretending to glance casually across the room, but her assumed nonchalance faded into a flare of unease and a burst of fright as her eyes met the waiting gaze.

He was sitting alone, just simply watching, his elbow on the table, his strong, arrogant chin resting on the long, curved fingers of his left hand, and the mocking smile on his face was not in any way assumed. Blue eyes with the hard glitter of diamonds held hers, and Merissa sat looking helplessly back.

He was dark, his hair heavy and black, his eyebrows winged like the devil himself, the straight nose, high cheek-bones and the insolent tilt to his head making him seem even more disturbing. The dark, handsome face was vividly intense against the white shirt beneath his black

dinner jacket, and there was no doubt that he knew he had
a compelling hold on her mind in those few seconds.

Merissa's lips parted unknowingly as a fluttering inside
her turned into a painful burning that flooded her face,
because there was no mistaking that look—she had seen it
before, the speculating look of the hunting male, a look that
began to strip her naked as his hard blue eyes narrowed to
vivid points of light. She had seen it all before, but she had
never felt like this. Her normal reaction to this kind of
scrutiny was disgust, her neat, hard shell covering her
effectively as contempt showed on her face. Now, though,
she was forlornly defenceless, and the contempt was all on
his face as he observed her fascinated awe.

He had cruel lips, firm and sensuous but carved into a
cruel mould that became more pronounced every second,
and Merissa felt a panic growing inside her that promised
to get out of control. For some reason, she felt close to tears
of alarm, and she actually jumped with fright when Hugh
slid back into his seat, his broad shoulders shielding her
from the hard blue eyes.

'There—not long, was I?' he asked with a little smile,
apparently noticing nothing amiss, probably because he
too looked just a little scared. At any rate, there was a line of
moisture on his top lip that he wiped away with an
impatient hand. 'I hope they're not going to be too long
with the food. We ordered straight away, it should be here
by now.' He sounded more uneasy than ever, his grumbling
a cover for some deeper feeling that had him in its grip. 'If
there's anything that annoys me it's waiting for service!'

'We've not been here five minutes,' Merissa said softly,
glad to have something to talk about because she was
utterly unable to make small talk. 'It's here anyway,' she
added as the waiter made his way deftly to their table.

Hugh's answer was merely a disgruntled sound, and she
was glad not to have to look up at him for a while as they
ate. She didn't want to look up at all. She wanted very
badly simply to go, preferably by magic carpet or inside a
thick smoke screen. She couldn't see the man now, but she

saw several people stop to talk to him as they passed, the men either downright friendly or deferential, the women with them all looking faintly flushed and bright-eyed. He was that kind of a man!

When they were at last ready to leave she took a deep breath, preparing herself to meet the sardonic gaze again, but he had already left, and she sighed aloud in relief. Ships that pass in the night! She wasn't sure what kind of a ship he was, but it would probably be crewed by pirates. He had the look about him.

Merissa wandered into the foyer to collect her wrap as Hugh stopped to speak again to the man who had attracted his attention before, his business acquaintance, but she wished she had stayed too as her eyes looked towards the doors that led to the street. He was there, the arrogant, sardonic gaze on her as she walked forward, and it took every bit of her training and pride to keep on walking, because this time he stopped in the doorway on his way out and looked across at her with open appraisal, his eyes moving over her face, her hair, her smooth, golden shoulders and onwards to examine every curve of her body, openly assessing her possibilities but with a contempt that hit out at her like a sharp slap across the separating space.

She couldn't go forward any more and she stopped, turning her face away, praying for Hugh to hurry out and join her, relieved when she felt the cool air from the outside as the man opened the door to leave.

'Beautiful, graceful and available.' His voice was as dark as his hair, as dark as the bronzed skin of his face, and she swung round angrily to answer this arrogant taunt, the words dying in her throat at the amused flash of his white teeth. 'All I need to know is—when? You want to answer now or wait until I see you again?'

Merissa was stunned, every bit of colour leaving her face, her ready tongue silent, her eyes wide and unbelieving, and he shrugged elegantly, his smile widening as he raised one hand in an insolent salute before disappearing into the night.

She couldn't get him out of her mind. Even next day as

she made her way to her agent's office, the dark, contemptuous face was still at the front of her mind, and she realised that through all her troubles nobody had ever managed to get under her guard like that. She remembered Hugh's look of surprise when he had come to join her as she stood lifelessly waiting the night before and she had been forced to tell him that she had a very sudden and fierce headache, although the truth was that a complete stranger had managed to penetrate her guard with a look and a few words where others had never succeeded since all her troubles had begun.

She knew she would never see him again, but still he lingered in her mind, another small brick to add to her growing wall of anxieties, and this morning she felt curiously dejected, friendless and vulnerable, her only safeguard the shell she had built around herself and the world and the only people she could trust in the world. There was her mother, there was Hugh and there was Clare Anders, her agent. She certainly did not need any stranger eyeing her over and acting like that. She had asked herself how he had acted, lingering on the small events with an almost morbid desire to remember every detail, and the only word she had been able to come up with was— threatening. She had felt threatened by the brilliance of his eyes, by the raw male look of him, by the assessing, contemptuous gaze. As they had stood in the foyer she too had had the chance to look him over as he had insolently studied her, and in spite of the tailored perfection of his clothes there had been a dangerous power to his body as if his casual stance by the door was a disguise to trap her into an ill-advised move. She thrust him out of her mind impatiently. Heavens, she had other problems, real ones, without letting her imagination paint frightening pictures of a man she would never see again.

'Merissa! I didn't expect to see you today!' Clare Anders swung round in surprise as Merissa walked into her office, but as usual her greeting was one of pleasure, and Merissa felt herself relax as she sat down at the other side of Clare's desk.

'I know you didn't expect me, Clare, but I was just wondering if anything had come up in the way of a job?'

'Nothing dear. It's the slack time, you know. Your Nash contract starts next week, though, doesn't it?'

'We start photographing on Monday, but I've got a whole week to kill. I hoped something had come up unexpectedly.'

'It rarely does, Merissa.' There was a certain hesitancy about Clare that gave Merissa the impression that there probably was something but that Clare was reluctant to mention it. It would probably be a job she would want to refuse.

'How's your mother?' Clare was clearly hedging, and Merissa smiled across at her. She doubted if anyone in the world understood her predicament as Clare understood it, and the enquiry about her mother was a very genuine one. Clare was a very powerful friend, the only one she had left except Hugh.

'Not too bad. One of her good days.' She had no need to pretend with Clare, because Clare knew the whole story, in fact it was Clare's long-standing friendship with the family that had led Merissa to becoming a photographic model when she had been forced to leave university half-way through her second year.

Clare looked worried as usual whenever any mention of Merissa's mother was made.

'The place where you live doesn't help very much, does it?' she began carefully. 'I could help out there, you know.'

'You've done enough, Clare. I'll sort it out eventually, and you know Mother—she's proud.'

'As proud as you are.' Clare smiled ruefully, her eyes lingering on the girl who sat with easy natural poise, her long slim legs crossed at the ankles, her beautifully shaped hands just a little tight on the arms of the chair, her eyes deliberately cheerful as usual.

If only Merissa had had a few more inches in height she

would have been able to climb to the top of the tree in the fashion world, but five feet six was not enough nowadays and Merissa's slender figure had curves in all the right places; one needed to be as thin as a beanpole to get to the top now.

'There's no need to do what you've set out to do, Merissa,' said Clare for the hundredth time, aware as she said it that the soft mouth would set into a determined line and the smiling eyes would cool. 'You're under no obligation, and neither is your mother.'

'We think we are, Clare,' Merissa said firmly, looking just as Clare had expected her to look when her troubles were mentioned. 'Mother still doesn't believe any of it and neither do I. At least we'll get everyone paid off, and then nobody will be able to say that Daddy left them holding the bag.'

Her chin tilted, and Clare knew the discussion had come to an end. Merissa had her father's tough spirit deep down, and although she had been forced to harden to survive in the fashion world, even though she had been obliged to stifle her natural gentleness and shyness, she would survive, Clare had no doubts about that. What worried her was whether or not Merissa would survive as she had been or whether the character she had been forced to play would finally take over, leaving the girl she had known since childhood as hard as she pretended to be now.

'Your father wouldn't have liked . . .' she pressed on anxiously, but Merissa had heard enough.

'He would have fought! I'm his daughter, and anyway, there's Mother to consider. If I could clear his name, she'd get better.'

'Merissa dear, asthma doesn't go just like that, it's hereditary.'

'Not always,' Merissa pointed out stubbornly. 'In her case, it was the shock and aftermath of Daddy's death, all the specialists agree, and anyway, Clare, I don't want to . . .'

'All right, all right,' sighed Clare. 'It's none of my business, I know. It's just that you spend every penny you earn on those appalling debts, and meanwhile your mother is in that awful house.'

'It's her idea,' Merissa pointed out, her eyes on her suddenly unsteady hands. 'I can't argue with her even if I wanted to.' She looked up and smiled brilliantly, hiding the misery and cares as best she could. 'Well, if there's nothing, I'll be on my way.'

'Wait a minute,' Clare sighed, realising that in her anxiety over Merissa's welfare she had brought back pain to the beautiful face and that worries that were normally well hidden were clouding the dark eyes. 'If you really need the money, there is a job.'

'I really need the money.' Merissa smiled, her face once more hopeful. 'Normal bills come in as well as—the other.'

'It's the new nightclub,' said Clare reluctantly, knowing the reception this information was going to get.

'A promotion? Oh, no! Is that all, Clare?'

'I'm afraid so. I know you won't normally do promotions, but this one is just a little different. It's at Fitzpatrick's— Grand Opening Gala and all that sort of thing.'

'I know. That's where all the people who are anybody will be going.'

'If you like,' Clare said smoothly. 'The pay is good, but you'd have to go on the catwalk and learn the choreography. There's a good bonus,' she added hastily, seeing the look of growing horror in the almond-shaped eyes. 'Five hundred pounds.'

'How many girls?' Merissa asked quickly, thinking about the electricity bill and stifling her distaste for this kind of thing, trying to keep her vivid imagination away from all the eyes that would be watching when the night came.

'All in all, ten,' Clare said evenly.

'Ten!' Merissa's face fell. 'Let's see, ten into five hundred goes . . .'

'Each,' said Clare with a little smirk. 'Five hundred each.'

'Each!' Merissa gaped at her. 'This promotion is going to

cost thousands if they're throwing their money about like that!'

'It is costing thousands,' Clare agreed, 'though I rather think the architect who designed it has had a hand in the scale of the promotion. Julian Forrest doesn't do things by halves, and I hear he was reluctant to be involved in a nightclub anyway. It's probably only because it's one of those lovely old Georgian buildings that he agreed to take on the conversion of the inside. He's probably making sure they don't imagine he'll ever do anything like that again. I hear he's a really tough customer.'

'Well, good for him,' murmured Merissa. 'I can't say I want the job, Clare, but then again, I need it. I'll survive.'

'You will, my pet,' Clare smiled. 'I'll be there in the audience, fingers crossed as usual at these events.

Merissa, however, was not quite so sure about surviving when the night came. She seemed to be surrounded by giants in their undies, but the thought didn't bring the usual smile to her face; her hard little shell had closed around her and she was too intent on the horror of her hair to be amused. The whole of her thick, shining hair had been sculptured into a shape, thick spikes frozen into place by lacquer. It stood above and around her head exactly like the Statue of Liberty, the final result sprayed with shocking colour. She was glad the make-up was heavy—she needed the mask, her eyelids sparkling with glitter at Clare's insistence.

Her outraged eyes met Clare's as she came in for a last-minute check, immaculately groomed and beautifuly dressed.

'Eye-catching!' remarked Clare, her face bland.

'Heart-stopping!' Merissa corrected. 'And I really do mean that. Thank goodness Mummy can't see this.'

'More eyeshadow,' Clare said smoothly, walking out.

'I take it that Mummy isn't in the audience to see her little pet perform?' one of the girls put in, sharpening her claws ready for an attack.

'No, thank God, she's in the Seychelles this season,'

Merissa snapped back in a hard and brittle voice. 'Your mascara is smudged,' she added, untruthfully, 'but I shouldn't bother, it blends beautifully with the dark circles under your eyes.'

She moved away as the tall girl bent anxiously to the mirror, and as usual, Merissa's heart was beating fast. She hated this, hated the whole life, hated to be sharp with people, but she had learned early on that she would never be left alone if she proved to be incapable of defending herself.

Her heart sank even further as she stepped into her outfit. There was very little of it and she would have centre stage. It was miles above her knees, it seemed, and almost showed her brief panties. One false move and the bodice would be dislodged, because only the thick, glittering rope of the belt seemed to be holding her together. She slipped into her shoes and fastened the straps, feeling the chill settle over her skin that anything of this sort brought on, a chill that grew as the music started.

She stepped out first, flanked by two of the others, both of them well over six feet tall, but their height only seemed to exaggerate her startling appearance and she knew that the gasp from the audience was for her. It was nearly her undoing.

For a second she faltered, and only the words whispered by the model who had spoken to her in the dressing-room kept her from darting back behind the curtains.

'Careful, your ladyship! We don't want anything to go wrong. Some of us have to earn a living.'

If only they knew! A sudden burst of anger filled her and she stepped forward and slightly in front of them. What did she care? She would make the audience gasp. The lights were too bright for her to see their faces anyway, and there were probably people here who were exactly like the people who had cheated her father and left her in this predicament. She moved forward on a wave of cold rage, improvising steps which fitted in spectacularly with the rehearsed movements of the others, lifting her out of the ordinary and bringing a loud burst of applause with a buzz of excited murmuring that almost drowned the music.

At the front of the catwalk she held her position as the others came out, and she made no attempt to keep up the glossy professional smile that clung to the faces of the other girls. She was a bizarre, smouldering beauty, dancing with an angry defiance that held the whole audience.

And then she saw the man. She could hardly miss him, he was with a party at a table nearest the catwalk edge, the same blue eyes sardonically on her face, the same near-disgust that had so puzzled her when she had seen him when she dined out with Hugh Goddard. His eyes ran over her scantily clad figure with the same speculation that had been there before, and for a second her steps faltered before she got a grip on her mind.

Surely he didn't recognise her! In this make-up, with this hairdo, she was totally different from the girl he had seen having dinner at an expensive restaurant, but she was held by the blue intensity of his eyes and she knew that he did recognise her and that for some unfathomable reason he wanted to taunt her.

She stared back defiantly, angrily, only her ear for rhythm and her flair for dancing keeping her feet going, her body moving. She no longer saw the crowded room, only the glitter of blue eyes that were slowly beginning to smile even before the carved lips moved in a half-smile of reluctant admiration. He raised his glass in arrogant salute, the others at his table laughing at the angry exchange that had taken place with no word spoken, and she snapped her eyes away, colour heating her skin at the almost possessive gleam in his eyes.

It seemed like years before she heard the sound she had been waiting for—the changed beat that signalled the end of the performance. The curtains slid back and they began to dance off the catwalk, Merissa leading.

Then one long leg shot out slyly to trip her as the girl she had put so firmly in her place sought retribution, and, feeling herself falling, Merissa knew she would soon be made to look a bigger fool than she already felt. She had always been nimble and athletic and her action was purely automatic. She flipped into a cartwheel and, mindless of the display of her scanty undics, cartwheeled off the stage and through the curtains to deafening applause and loud whistles.

She turned, white-faced and angry, as the others came in, but she had no chance to speak, because the others were just as angry.

'It's lucky for us that Merissa can do stunts like that,' one of them burst out sharply, 'otherwise we could all have forgotten the bonus!'

'Clare Anders doesn't miss a trick like that,' another added. 'I should start looking for another agency tomorrow if I were you.'

There was an unusual quiet and Merissa was left in peace in the angry and uneasy silence. Clare took on very few models and she certainly missed nothing at all, and Merissa was suddenly guilt-filled. Maybe if she had never answered when the girl had spoken so spitefully this would never have happened; she had become so used to protecting herself that she gave no one an inch nowadays. Her small exchange with the girls had brought on this whole episode, and she was suddenly tired of it all. She walked to the shower, ignoring the fact that they were all now going out to circulate among the people in the nightclub, part of the job. She didn't care any more about the bonus, and her eyes met Clare's as she walked into the room a little later to find Merissa restored to normal, her hair washed and dried into the usual heavy fall of shining glory.

'I can't face anything else, Clare,' she said flatly, and was relieved to see Clare's nod of understanding.

'No matter, love. I think you've done your full share out there tonight. I've collected your bonus, they're paying that in cash—and stop worrying, you were great! Brilliant innovation! If you'd fallen we would merely have had a farce; now the whole thing is the talk of the evening. Leave whenever you like.'

Merissa turned to the mirror after she had pulled on her pale green trousers and heavy matching sweater. She was still tanned from an assignment in the Canary Islands two weeks ago and her only concession to make-up was a pale pink lipstick. She felt a little more secure now that her normal image looked back at her, and she pulled on her high-heeled boots before fastening a thick belt securely round her slender waist and picking up the heavy bag that held her make-up and drier, the tools of her trade.

'You've made a name for yourself tonight, my girl,' Clare told her softly, her eyes searching Merissa's troubled face.

'Well, don't tell me what the name is—please,' Merissa quipped flippantly, taking the five hundred pounds in crisp new bills that Clare held out to her. 'I feel as if I brought the whole thing on myself. I can't seem to hold my tongue when anyone makes a dig at me. I used to hurt over it—I still do, I suppose, but now I just drive straight back at them. Don't get rid of her, Clare, it was as much my fault as . . .'

'Hardly!' Clare stated, with raised eyebrows. 'I know what goes on in the dressing-room very often. I was a model myself, remember? Once out there, though, professionalism is expected, and if it's not there then I'm not interested any more.'

It was true. Merissa knew that, but her guilt did not lessen, and she stepped back into the bright lights with Clare feeling miserable and downcast, a little spark of gratitude inside her when she saw to her surprise the tall, fair figure of Hugh striding towards her.

'Damn!' he grinned, taking her arm and nodding pleasantly at Clare. 'You changed back into the princess. I was hoping to get a closer look at the witch!'

'Hugh! What are you doing here?' Merissa smiled up at him and he slid a comforting arm around her shoulders.

'I'm here for the opening. If you remember, I asked you out tonight, but you said you were working. This is where we were going; luckily this is where we both ended up. I never expected to get to see you perform. Wow!' His eyes had a different look, and her heart sank like lead. Hugh was a friend, an old friend, and she couldn't take on any speculating looks from him. It was not only her lack of height that kept her off the catwalk, it was precisely the look that was in Hugh's eyes now that she avoided by being a photographic model and working in the peace of a studio.

Her heart sank even further at the sight of the two men who were coming across the room towards them, and she gripped Hugh's arm with a quick burst of fear. One of the men was the nightclub owner, but the other man had brilliant eyes, blue eyes that had lost their smile and were now filled with the contempt she had seen before.

'Fabulous, Clare!' Robert Greenway grasped Clare's hand and shook it vigorously. 'The next nightclub I open, you do the promotion—providing this little lady is there, of course.' He beamed at Merissa, but Clare knew her well and stepped in effortlessly.

'She won't be, though, she's not that kind of a model. She only does photographic work; tonight's effort was a favour to me.'

'I won't be a minute, there's somebody I need to see over there.' Hugh pulled away from Merissa's tight grasp and she watched him walk off quickly, stunned at the look on his face. The tight fear was suddenly back in his eyes, and she saw the blue-eyed stranger turn and watch him walk off, his own face also tight, but not with fear.

Clare and Robert Greenway were in the middle of an animated business discussion, and she turned to say goodbye, anxious to be out of the range of the clear blue eyes, but it wasn't going to be that easy.

'So you're a photographic model?' His voice was as dark as she remembered it and she barely glanced up as she nodded, unable to answer him at all. 'What do you do, work in the nude?'

Merissa's head shot up at this taunt, colour flooding her face, and her anger rising to cover her little fear, her own lips tightening in annoyance.

'Only when I'm hot, and that's usually when I'm cooking dinner!' She glared at him, her cheeks flaring with colour, and he laughed delightedly, the blue eyes alight with amusement as one strong hand brushed her cheek. She almost sprang away from the touch. It had sent ripples of unease through her, the light touch of an electric current not on full power, and she suddenly had a vivid picture of what it must be like when he really touched a woman, her colour flaring again at the thought of the aggressive sexuality about him, something he wore easily, as easily as he wore the superbly tailored suit.

'Hey!' His voice was smokily soft, his compelling eyes smiling. 'I asked for that and I surely got it. I wasn't about to slap you, so there's no need to jump like a frightened cat. How old are you?'

'It's none of your business!' Merissa was having a struggle and her eyes searched anxiously for escape, but Clare was talking business to Greenway and Hugh had disappeared into the crowd.

'All right, you're twenty-two—no, twenty-three. Now tell me your name.'

'I have no intention of telling you anything!' Merissa, realising that she was on her own, collected her shell belatedly and struggled into it. 'Normally I don't even talk to people who force their attentions on me. At the moment I'm merely being polite.'

'Are you merely polite to Goddard? I somehow doubt that. You're pretty typical of the kind of woman he runs around with, although you're a little young. Still, you've probably got all the experience he likes—you were certainly not bashful tonight on that catwalk. Did you get all the acclaim you like? I can assure you that everyone got their money's worth, especially those on our table.'

'I came to do a job and I did it!' Merissa shook the crisp notes under his nose. 'I came for the bonus and I earned it! Now will you kindly go away?'

'No!' The hardness left his voice again and his eyes were almost hypnotic. 'I want to see you again. I want to take you away from Goddard, so when is it going to be?'

'Look, I—I don't know, you. I don't want to know you.

To me you're just like any other man who thinks that
because I'm a model he can pester me and make
suggestions. I'm not interested!'

'I'll take you home.' He reached for her heavy bag, but
she got there first and swung it out of his reach, her eyes a
little wild as she stared into the blue of his.

'Don't you ever listen!'

'Hardly ever,' he assured her, his hands sliding into his
pockets as he stood squarely in front of her. 'I have a
tremendous drive when I'm after something I want. I'll
give you two guesses about what I want now.'

Merissa dodged round him and ran, almost bumping
into Hugh, who was apparently waiting for her at the edge
of a crowd of people, and she couldn't for the life of her
understand why he hadn't come and rescued her before
now. Clearly he had long ago finished talking to whoever
had attracted his attention.

'What's up?' He took the bag and was apparently quite
happy to leave, although if she hadn't been there she was
sure he had intended to stay for the evening.

'Nothing! I just want to get out of here. I've been talking
to the most—irritating man.' She had been going to say 'the
most revolting man', but she bit hard on her lip as she
realised that she didn't think that at all. The naked sexual
aggression had frightened her, but it had also excited her in
a way that she had never felt before.

'I noticed.' Hugh was subdued, even angry. 'I was just
coming back to get you.'

He hadn't been, she was certain of that, and she glanced
sideways at him from beneath her thick lashes as they went
towards the car park. Something, somebody had within the
last few days upset Hugh, and she suddenly wondered
about the man with brilliant eyes.

'Who is that man, Hugh?' she asked with as much
nonchalance as she could muster.

'What man?' He was opening his car door and kept his
face averted. 'You didn't bring your car, did you?'

'No.' Merissa shook her head but persisted with her

question. 'Hugh, who is that man who was talking to me?'

'I've honestly no idea, love. Just another of the kind who hang around places like that trying to pick up girls, I expect. There are plenty of that type around.'

There were, but somehow this man didn't fit, although he had certainly tried to pick her up—twice! As to Hugh not knowing him, she thought he did, and she suddenly looked at him with new eyes. The type of woman he runs around with, that was what the man had said. Merissa realised she knew very little about Hugh, even though he had been a small part of her life for so long. All at once she felt uneasy with him, and it wasn't a nice feeling; she had been accustomed to thinking of him as an old friend, somebody her father had approved of, somebody who had stuck it out when most of the other so-called friends had deserted her and her mother, unable to face the scandal. Damn the blue-eyed devil! He was putting disquieting thoughts into her head that she could well do without. She had enough to worry about.

Her mother was waiting up for her as usual, and Merissa entertained her with a run down of the evening's events as they sat later, cosily wrapped in their dressing-gowns, although she never mentioned the man or Hugh's suddenly odd behaviour. She counted out the money that she had picked up and put aside a pile of notes.

'Out of this we can pay the immediate bills,' she said firmly, 'and this,' pointing to the separate pile, 'is a new coat for you.'

'Oh, no! Darling, you're so good, but I know you have to keep up appearances in your job. You must use it for new clothes yourself.'

'No way!' declared Merissa. According to the man who kept bobbing up into her life, she needed no clothes at all. She found her face flushing at the memory and found her anger rising too. It really was ridiculous getting so heated about a complete stranger, but he was definitely lingering in her head like a bad dream. 'I've got enough clothes for ages. You go to town tomorrow and get a nice new coat.

We'll get off really early. Last word!'

'Shouldn't we use it to . . .' her mother began anxiously, but Merissa cut in determinedly.

'No, we shouldn't use it to . . .' she said. 'They can wait a while now. We have to live too, if you can call this living.' She looked round with a sigh. 'I'm sick of you being here. You've never lived in a place like this in your whole life, and if it wasn't for those debts I could get us a place in the country. You're practically confined to the house. I hate it when you go even one step outside without me. Every morning I expect to find that my car has been vandalised, it's like living on the edge of a jungle.'

'We'll move when Daddy's name is cleared.' Her mother's voice was as usual, firm in this resolution. 'We've got it nice inside with some of our old things.'

It was true—they had, Merissa thought, looking round at the comfortable chairs in bright covers, the polished tables, but her father's face swam into her mind and she felt a wave of guilt that she was unable to get her mother to a better place, a more healthy place. She had taken on all the responsibility, but sometimes she was aware of her burden. With so much depending on her it was a weight that she found hard to carry at times like these. Her mother was still young, in her early forties, but she had given up trying to cope when Merissa's father had died. Her only firm grip on life seemed to be her determination to clear his name and pay off the debts that had blackened it, her steady avowal that it was all some monstrous mistake her only hope. It was impossible to do anything but go along with her, and any argument could bring on a frightening attack of asthma. Meanwhile they lived here, making ends meet but only just, proudly struggling on.

Merissa did not normally feel so depressed, though. It was something to do with the man she had seen, his unjust remarks; his contempt had got under her skin and hurt her. She was thankful she would never see him again, and she resolved never to do another promotion as long as she lived. Better to be working in the peace and quiet of a studio well out of the way of any interfering stranger.

CHAPTER TWO

THE following Monday saw the beginning of the Nash contract, and Merissa was working with Philip Swift, a young and vigorous photographer who was rising like a star in his profession and who liked to work with her.

They were making up the new autumn catalogue, months ahead of time as normal, and Merissa loved the clothes. They were well designed, expensive and in lovely jewel colours that suited her clear, tanned skin, her dark eyes.

Each change of clothes needed a new hairstyle, and she forgot every worry as she used her skill before the camera and her wits in front of the mirror, each new innovation bringing a critical glance from Philip followed by a sharp nod of approval.

'We'll call it a day, Merissa,' Philip told her after three hours. 'I'm dropping, and I know you must be too, although I never hear you complain. Nine o'clock tomorrow? We'll do the outside shots, weather permitting.'

He turned to his equipment and she hurried to the dressing-room at the side of the studio, slipping out of the fine woollen dress and putting it carefully on a hanger. Philip didn't like to linger when he had finished, and she washed quickly, making her face up lightly, standing in her pale lemon undies as she bent to the mirror. The lacy bra and matching camiknickers were another expensive bonus from a job. She had a whole set of undies and night wear from a lingerie advertisement she had done earlier in the year, and she could never have afforded to buy this sort of thing for herself. At the time she had wished the bonus had been in cash—for the usual reasons—but now she was glad it hadn't been. She could not afford to be shabby in her job,

24

and she was becoming more and more reluctant to spend money on clothes.

The sharp tap on the door had her nearly jumping out of her skin, and she turned startled dark eyes that registered their relief as Clare walked in.

'Merissa, sorry! Did I startle you? I've been so busy today and I knew you'd be here,' she explained. 'There's a job for you starting straight after this one, beginning next week.'

Merissa's joy turned to fury and embarrassment, however, when a tall, dark-haired figure appeared behind Clare, propping himself comfortably against the open door, his lean face wryly amused, his brilliant blue eyes skimming over her scantily clad figure with open enjoyment.

'What—how dare you!' She instantly slipped into her defensive shell, her eyes flashing with anger as Clare turned, startled in her turn, to look with shocked disapproval at the man who had so clearly followed her in without her knowledge.

'Why the startled maiden act?' he enquired sardonically, his eyes roaming over her with a kind of fierce pleasure that made her colour and her temper rise both at the same time, 'I thought models were used to being half naked—all girls together.'

Merissa advanced on him furiously. It was useless to snatch up her clothes now like the startled maiden he suggested, she would have to cross the dressing-room under those eyes, so she might as well cross towards him.

'Somewhere along the line you've missed out in your education!' she snapped furiously. 'I'll tell you though, quite categorically, you are not a girl! And now that we have that settled—get out!' She stared into the smiling, taunting eyes and then slammed the door hard, and he let her have her way, stepping back into the studio as the door swung viciously shut.

'Now that has torn it!' Clare was looking a little red-faced herself. 'That was the man offering the job. I really don't know what he was thinking about, following me in here.'

'Well, I know,' raged Merissa, colour still high on her face, the skin of her legs tingling still from the comprehensive scrutiny of those devilish eyes. 'And I refuse the job!'

'All right, I'll tell him,' Clare said worriedly. 'I can understand your annoyance, Merissa, but honestly, he's a really nice man, he's . . .'

'I don't want to know who he is or what he is!' snapped Merissa, still trembling from his terrifying appraisal. 'I'm sorry, Clare, but I wouldn't work for that particular man if he paid in gold doubloons!'

'He probably could,' Clare put in wryly. 'He's rolling in it.'

'May he choke in it!' Merissa muttered and Clare shrugged resignedly.

'I'll tell him. Pop in to see me next week when you're feeling better.'

It was only when Clare had gone that Merissa found the time and breath to realise that she was in two states of mind. Frightened, she was all of that, but to her growing shame, she was excited. There had been people who had pursued her for a while during her short career, but never quite like this, never a man like that, never with such outright and naked sexual approval on his face. He was not all he seemed, some inner instinct told her; he was an enemy, her survival instinct told her that, too, but she couldn't help the shivering feeling that shuddered over her when he looked at her, and she flushed anew with outright disgust at the way her body ignored her mind. He was probably some hideous nightclub freak, probably married too. The thought renewed her temper and she dressed angrily. If she ever saw him again . . .!

'No car, Merissa?' Philip Swift asked as they stepped out on to the pavement later together.

'No. I don't like bringing it into central London at this time of the day. The Tube will do fine.'

'Give you a lift?' he enquired pleasantly, but she shook

her head. The walk would restore her temper and calm her shattered nerves. She had always to be sure that her mother saw no sign of tiredness or turmoil on her face when she got home. She needed the journey today more than ever.

Philip nodded in farewell and she walked round the corner, almost bumping into the man who lounged beside the Mercedes Sports, his blue eyes cool and watchful on her startled face, his own face tightening into near anger at the wave of frustrated fury that drove the shock from her dark eyes.

'May I offer you a lift, then?' he asked with carefully controlled politeness as she stopped in front of him, having no alternative as he was blocking the pavement and standing straight and tall in the way.

'No, thank you! I've thrown you out of my dressing-room and sent you the message—no, in clear capital letters. I have no further words for your ears, except to ask you with as much civility as I can muster to please leave me alone and keep out of my way.'

'I've never been thrown out by a woman before,' he said in a deceptively soft voice. 'If Mrs Anders hadn't been there, maybe I would have grappled with you when you were in your fighting gear. Maybe I should have done, after all.'

Merissa's face flushed hotly and she raised dark, angry eyes to meet his clear blue gaze, but before she could speak he went on,

'Look, I need you for an important job. Do you mind if we bury the hatchet and talk? Maybe we got off on the wrong foot, and if we did, then I'm prepared to say I'm sorry.'

'I don't want your job or your apologies,' she said quietly, hitching her bag up on to her shoulder. 'I just want to be left alone to get on with my own affairs, and you don't figure in them at all. Now, please let me pass.'

His hand came to her arm, though, firm but not hurtful, but with enough strength to keep her exactly where she stood, and there was a great deal more strength there if he needed to use it, she could tell that.

'Wait a minute, you prickly little hedgehog,' he said quietly. 'I'm not joking. I really need you.'

'So you intimated, the other times we met,' she flashed at him regretting it immediately because it produced a flush of colour on her own face and only brought amusement to his.

'I've sinned, I know,' he admitted with an odd look in his eyes, 'but I had other things on my mind then, not really you, as it happens. This is a business deal, straight down the middle. What about it?'

'No!' It was hard to meet the eyes that now smiled coaxingly into hers, but she did it, tightening her face and managing to make her soft lips look hard and bitter. 'You're wasting your time—and mine!'

'Very well,' he stepped back to allow her to pass, 'I tried to be nice, I really did. It's not an attitude that really suits me, but then I think I managed it fairly well. OK, young lady, have it your way. Goodbye.'

He simply got into his car and moved out into the traffic with an expertise that she envied, manoeuvring into the only tiny gap available and sweeping off with smooth speed. She would have had to wait several minutes to pull out into that lot, and she stared after him until the car had disappeared from sight.

She was astonished by the way he had simply capitulated and, contrarily, she was a little disappointed. He didn't look like a man who would take no for an answer, but he had done. She walked off with her head held high, although there was no one in particular to see her. It was a habit.

She had lots of habits now, she realised as she sat on the train on her way home. She had acquired a temper, a vicious tongue and a hard, brittle shell that threatened to become permanent. She had never really looked at her pretended self closely; her act was a cloak she stepped into every day of her working life, shedding it when necessary. Had it really been necessary to fly into a rage when he had come to her dressing-room door. After all, he could hardly have realised what he would see when he got here. Still, he had looked at her with that barely concealed contempt and that arrogant look of sexuality. Merissa's cheeks flushed as she remembered. It seemed that he found her distasteful but also tempting. It was a personality she didn't fit into at all, yet he had looked at her like that from the moment he had seen her. His words about Hugh came back to her mind. Was all this something to do with Hugh and nothing to do with her at all? Was this man some enemy of Hugh Goddard and she merely a pawn in the game? Certainly there had been times when he had appeared almost to relent, then the hard eyes had been soft and smiling, the dark cool voice almost gentle. Heavens, she was utterly muddled—and what did it matter? She would never see him again now anyway. She looked out of the window and made a determined effort to get him right out of her mind.

Although the Nash Collection was photographed and finished by mid-week, Merissa put off going to see Clare until Friday. Somehow there was a worrying crack in her shell and she was uneasy even about facing Clare. She need not have been, though.

'I've got the most fantastic news for you!' cried Clare, bubbling with enthusiasm. 'On Monday at ten-thirty you have a photographic session with—wait for it—Derrick Lean!' She sat back and watched Merissa's face, a thoroughly smug satisfaction on her own. 'This is your great chance, Merissa, the big one!'

Merissa could believe it. Derrick Lean was just about the most skilful and famous fashion photographer in the country, in Europe, actually. To work with him was the dream of any model who wanted to rise to the top, and she did; she had to.

'The advertisement you're doing is for the new shopping centre, the one that's been going up for the past six months.'

'That's the one where every shop and boutique is going to be filled with things too expensive to buy, isn't it?'

'That's the one, well out of the reach of the common herd,' affirmed Clare, looking quite pleased about it. 'There'll be a restaurant there that will become world-famous, if I'm not mistaken. Everybody with any push is trying to get hold of the property there, and it's really beautiful!'

'I haven't seen it since they started. Isn't it a place by what's-his-name?'

'Julian Forrest,' Clare nodded, 'and it's typical of the buildings he designs. It fits into the surroundings as if it had been there for at least a century, and inside—the luxury!' She cast her eyes up and held up her hands in awe.

'I—I'm advertising it?' asked Merissa, awestricken herself. 'Is this an audition?'

'No, you've got the job. Monday is the session, and it's not going to take long.'

'Oh!' This time Merissa's exclamation was disappointment. A few hours wouldn't pay off any debts, even if it was with Derrick Lean.

'The pay is fantastic, the future bright,' Clare said sternly as she saw Merissa's face fall. 'You get two thousand pounds.'

'I get what?' Merissa actually jumped to her feet, and Clare smiled smugly, pointing to the seat which Merissa sank into.

'Two thousand pounds. You heard.'

'For a few hours? I can't believe it,' Merissa whispered in awe. 'Only the best and most well known models . . .'

'Julian Forrest asked for you,' Clare assured her. 'He must have seen your work somewhere. Of course, I'll want my commission as usual,' she grinned, 'but if I were to be honest, I haven't had to do a thing to get this job for you, it just appeared.'

'It's like a fairytale,' murmured Merissa.

'Which brings me to the big point,' Clare announced, emphasising the words. 'You have to look like a lady—and I do mean a lady.'

'Don't I always?' grinned Merissa.

'Not when you're letting that hard little shell creep around you,' Clare asserted firmly. 'You're to look older, sophisticated but sweetly feminine. The orders were very explicit.'

'Consider it done,' Merissa pronounced. 'What do I wear?'

'The garment will be provided,' said Clare as if she was repeating a line she had learned. 'Do you want to hear the best part?'

'There's more?' Merissa asked breathlessly.

'More,' Clare assured her. 'Your final, chosen shot will be going up on every available hoarding in London. Great big coloured shots of you. Your face will be on every passing bus, you'll be as well known as a television personality by the end of the month. When the new centre is discussed, your face will spring into every mind. People will be falling all over themselves to give you work, and we only accept the best thereafter,' she finished firmly.

'On every hoarding,' whispered Merissa, and suddenly burst into laughter. 'I'll need a disguise!'

'Maybe,' Clare conceded thoughtfully. 'Just remember to leave off your normal disguise when you do the job. You don't need your shell any more, Merissa, from now on you can call the tune yourself, you can work with whoever you like.'

'If all goes well,' Merissa reminded her a trifle wistfully. Things did not normally go well.

'Be your real self, it will go well,' said Clare reassuringly. 'The rest is up to me. I'll get you the work, and very soon your problems will be over.'

'Not very soon, Clare,' Merissa reminded her. 'The problems are the debts, and they're stacked knee-deep. Still,' she added happily, 'any work that comes from this will be better paid, won't it?'

'You'd better believe it,' snorted Clare in a determined way.

'I wonder what Julian Forrest is like?' Merissa asked rather dreamily as she finally got to the door on her way out. 'I'd love to meet him. Do you think I will, Clare?'

'I should think so,' Clare said offhandedly, turning back to her desk. 'You'll probably get on like a house on fire,' she added, 'but whatever, don't forget that your future hangs on this one job, not to mention your mother's,' she added unfairly and deliberately.

'I know. Don't worry,' said Merissa with a little smile.

'I'll ring you on Sunday with the final arrangements,' Clare promised as she left, and as Merissa closed the door, Clare crossed her fingers and raised her eyes heavenwards. 'Please, just this once, let her remember that she's a beautiful, gentle and kind girl,' she prayed as she looked at the ceiling.

Derrick Lean put Merissa at her ease at once. He had arranged for a huge stretch of green canvas to hide them from the road and any interested spectators, so that to all intents and purposes they seemed to be working in a great outdoor studio. And the building was beautiful. If anyone had told Merissa she could have found a shopping centre beautiful, she would have laughed, but this one she could hardly stop looking at. From the outside, it looked old, elegantly designed, with the symmetry and balance of the other old buildings around it, but inside, once the marble open precinct was crossed, once the slender Doric columns had been passed, there was the twentieth century at its very best.

One of the boutiques had been opened so that Merissa would have privacy in which to change, and as she came back, her eyes still wandering over the high ceilings, the slender columns, she found the photographer waiting, his three assistants at the ready.

'Impressive, isn't it?' said Derrick Lean, nodding towards the rather grand and certainly palatial surroundings.

'Beautiful,' Merissa confessed dreamily, her head thrown back as she studied the grandeur of the place.

'So are you,' the photographer remarked with no flattery in his voice but just a quiet, matter-of-fact announcement that caused her no embarrassment. 'I hear you're good in front of a camera too, and very easy to work with. So am I. Let's see you perform. Just remember that you're Lady Agatha.'

She had no time for nerves, he had started, the camera clicking before she could catch breath, and within minutes she was enjoying herself.

The surroundings, the clothes she wore and her odd feeling of happiness combined to bring out her old self. There was no need to act, her face was composed and serene, she was sure of herself.

She had blown her hair off her face in a casual manner, her fringe parted in the middle and flicked back, choosing her style with flair as soon as she saw the dress. It was white, long and looked frighteningly expensive, the low halter front hanging from a thin strap, the back sweeping down to her waist, and whoever had chosen the sandals evidently knew her size and had perfect taste. They were silver kid, comfortable and very high-heeled. The silver bracelet and necklace had also been there ready for her. The whole outfit showed off her golden tan, and she felt wonderful.

'A very expensive lady,' Derrick Lean murmured as he darted round her, following her movements rather than arranging her, giving her credit for her natural ability.

If this is earning money, please let it go on happening! thought Merissa, smiling to herself.

'No smiles, Lady Agatha!' Derrick ordered as she leaned against a slender column.

'She's fabulous!' put in one of the assistants in admiration.

'Down, Rover!' ordered the master. 'Get the next camera ready, keep your eye on the fan.'

The fan in question was blowing a gentle breeze that swirled around Merissa and moulded her dress to her body as she passed it. He was letting her wander at will, and she worked very well under these circumstances—in fact, it was nothing like work at all.

'That's it!' he said suddenly, straightening up and handing his camera to the ready hand of one of his acolytes. 'Finished.'

'Finished?' Merissa couldn't help the little exclamation of disappointment, and he grinned, clearly pleased.

'Now that, from a model, is praise,' he admitted. 'However, a good half of the reason for the early finish is you. You're a very clever model, Merissa. I'd really like to work with you again.'

'Oh, thank you!' She felt breathless, heady with this praise, and her haughty Lady Agatha look disappeared as her pleasure flooded her face with colour and brightened her eyes.

'Pretty little thing,' the great man murmured. 'I'll be in touch.'

He was already walking off, leaving, and she asked in a rather panicky voice,

'Mr Lean, what about the clothes, the jewellery? Do I hand them to my agent?'

'Oh, no. Sorry. Apparently they're the bonus. You keep them.'

'But they're too expensive,' she whispered, quite shocked.

'That's what the man said,' he laughed. 'Tell her the things are a bonus—his very words, as I remember. You'll have to go out on the town in them,' he added in amusement as he walked away.

Merissa stood stunned after he had gone and then gathered herself hastily together as a man, clearly some kind of security guard, sauntered on to the precinct with the clear intention of locking up her improvised dressing-room.

She was still stunned as she stepped out on to the street later, the dress carefully folded in her bag, the sandals lovingly packed, the jewellery safely hidden in her handbag, but her dreamlike trance faded as she saw who was parked at the bottom of the steps and the well remembered colour began to rise on her face. Oh, no, not again! She tried to ignore him, looking over his head instead of directly at him as she walked down the flight of elegant steps. She might as well have never bothered.

'Well done,' he remarked evenly. 'Transformed by a dress and the expression on your face. Clever girl!'

'You had no business to be there!' she snapped, realising that he must have been somewhere inside watching. The dress was now well hidden and his eyes were skimming over her mauve trouser suit, not with the now expected speculation, though, but with a hardness that was businesslike and in its own way equally frightening.

'I had every right, Miss Troy,' he assured her. 'You've spent the last two hours working for me, and your pay is right here.'

He handed her a thick envelope, and it was securely in her hands before she could stop him. All she could do was stare at him in silence, and he smiled without any humour.

'Your agent said you like cash,' he added scathingly, 'so that's what you have—cash.'

'I haven't been working for you!' Merissa suddenly burst out, praying it wasn't true. He was more alarming now in this new attitude than he had been before when he had looked at her so sensuously. Now he was cold as ice and determination was written all over his face. 'Julian Forrest picked me himself! My agent told me so!'

'And she was quite right: I did pick you myself. I just suspected that your face might be the one to advertise the centre. You certainly know your job, and I should think one of those shots will soon be all over London. However, the job was by way of a test. I have another more important job for you, now that you've shown what you can do.'

'I had no idea you were Julian Forrest,' she said, angrily quiet. 'If I'd known, I would never have taken the job.'

'Not even for the money?' he enquired in a disbelieving voice. 'I gained the impression from your agent that money figured largely in your life.'

Not for the reasons you seem to think, she wanted to shout at him, but she struggled to keep her temper as the cool blue eyes watched her closely. He seemed to be a different man today, in fact he had really been rather different when he had invaded her dressing-room. The hunting male attitude was gone, and although it was not now so very obvious she had the distinct impression that the contempt had deepened. He was simply keeping it under wraps because he wanted her for a job.

'Think whatever you wish,' she said quietly. 'I've done

the job for you now and there's nothing I can do to undo it. So thank you for the pay and goodbye. Oh,' she added as a thought struck her, 'as I shan't be seeing you again, I'll give you the clothes and the jewellery now. I can't think of a single place where I could wear them, and in any case, they're far too expensive to be given as a bonus. My greed does have a limit.'

She dived into her bag, but the hand on her wrist stopped her, gripping like steel and making any further move impossible.

'You'll need them for the job I have for you!' he rasped. 'Those and plenty more like them!'

'Except that I won't be doing the job, Mr Forrest,' Merissa advised him tightly. 'I've been tricked into working for you once, but wild horses wouldn't get me to work for you again.'

'Why?' The casual question almost threw her off balance for a second, but she was used to making quick recoveries.

'I don't like you. I don't trust you. I don't like your attitude to me either, and I don't enjoy being pursued by aggressive men with that—look in their eyes!'

He stood frowning down at her for a second, then shook his head as if he were clearing his thoughts.

'I did not have the look in my eyes that you imagine, and my reasons were not what you imagine either. My reasons also are my private business. This is a job, pure and simple.'

'Indeed! Well, as you clearly think I'm not really pure and as I'm certainly not simple, forget it.'

'How would you like it if the photographs you did today were confined to the first dustbin that I see? How would you like it if Derrick Lean forgot entirely about your small and insignificant existence? He's a great friend of mine.'

End of another small dream, Merissa thought bitterly, but nothing of her disappointment showed on her face as she looked up at him.

'You must do as you wish,' she said coolly as she turned away. 'I'll be going now. I've earned the money you gave me, and as you so rightly say, that's all I'm interested in.

There are other photographers. I already work regularly.'
She started to move away, but his arm shot out and
clamped round her waist, making further movement
impossible.

'I want you for a job and you're going to do it!' he grated
savagely, glaring down into her astonished eyes, seeing the
fear there and looking thoroughly satisfied with it.

'How dare you! Let me go!' Merissa cried hotly,
struggling wildly. 'This is called assault, Mr Forrest! Let
me go!'

How was it that when right was on her side there wasn't a
soul around? She was beginning to be really frightened, it
even came into her mind that he might be mad. Perhaps
that was the feeling she had had when he had looked at her
before, the warning you were supposed to get when you
met someone who wasn't quite all there.

Relief flooded through her as the security guard came
down the steps with measured tread, and she could hardly
believe it when he spoke to Julian Forrest and completely
ignored the fact that the man was holding a struggling
captive.

'Everything locked up safely, Mr Forrest.'

'Thanks, Sam. Keep an eye on things.' He was so calm, so
sure of himself, not in any way out of breath, although
Merissa's wild struggles were leaving her panting. He
touched his peaked cap and moved off.

'Sam!' Merissa raised her voice, but he just ignored her,
grinning at Julian Forrest, who raised his eyes heavenwards and opened the car door. The fool thought they were
having a lovers' quarrel! She opened her mouth to shout
louder, but she was in the car, the door shut and her
assailant sitting beside her before she could react to the
impossibility of it all.

'Now we talk!' he rasped, locking the doors electronic-
ally, 'and if you continue to make a scene, I'll drive out into
the country and drop you into the first pond I see!'

'There was no scene until you started manhandling me!'

she shouted, mindless of the volume of her voice in the close confines of the car.

'I'm quite sure you're used to scenes,' he bit out, wincing at the power of her voice in the small space. 'I want you for a job and I intend that the job shall be done! The job is respectable, important to me, comfortable, and the pay is fifteen thousand pounds on completion!'

'Fifteen thousand pounds!'

'To the penny!' he growled, his eyes losing their anger and filling with derision. 'I somehow thought money would be the magic word.'

She wasn't listening, wasn't even bothering about the insulting tone or the look in his eyes. Fifteen thousand pounds plus the two she already had, plus a chance to work with Derrick Lean. She began to see the debts dwindling, a cottage in the country, her mother's face healthy.

'What's the job?' she asked quietly as he drove off, a look of smug disdain on his face.

'I want you to be my fiancée,' Julian Forrest announced matter-of-factly, his expression not altering, all his attention on the road.

'Let me out! The next bus stop will do!' She was furious as well as panic-stricken. He was mad, he had to be. 'The joke's over, Bluebeard! Pull over or I'll break the window with my shoe!'

'Carry on,' he invited quietly. 'It can't be done, but it will occupy you nicely and any damage to the car I'll take off your final pay.'

Merissa made a lunge for the steering wheel, but an arm like an iron band blocked her and he looked angry enough to really scare her.

'An accident may damage that beautiful and unusual face,' he reminded her with quiet anger, 'and then only your mother would want you. Certainly there would be no further point in offering you the job, and Derrick Lean's interest would be quite dead.'

That frightened her into silence and stillness, and she sat

trembling as the powerful sports car slid in and out of the city traffic.

'You can stop trembling,' he said curtly after a few minutes. 'I'm not driving you to my quiet flat—I don't even own one. The idea of ravishing you doesn't appeal in the slightest. I'd need cotton wool in my ears and a blindfold. I'm quite sure your beauty is very much skin-deep only.

'Where are we going?' whispered Merissa shakily, shocked to realise that his words were hurting her and terrified by his actions. It was unthinkable that she had been tricked into working for him when she had refused, that sort of thing didn't happen, but it was even more unthinkable that she had been forced into his car and driven off against her will, and it was obvious that he didn't even like her. Why the job? She glanced at him from beneath thick lashes. Maybe it was for some criminal reason? She looked away quickly and repeated her question when he never bothered to answer.

'You may not have noticed, in your maidenly panic,' he remarked drily, 'but in fact, we're going round in circles. When you've recovered your wits sufficiently enough to give me directions, I'm taking you home. To your home!'

She didn't want that. She didn't want him to see the place where her mother was forced to live. Already his contempt was overwhelming her and she could do without any more of it, and as to the job, once she was out of the car Julian Forrest could start looking for another accomplice.

'Well?' he prompted testily when she kept silent, but she still did not answer. He had her feeling trapped, in fact there was something about him that definitely spoke of the predator. She had been pursued, tracked down, cornered. He was a complete stranger and he had followed her trail for days. It seemed like years ago that she had seen him in that restaurant when she was with Hugh, and since then he had slowly followed her until now he actually had her cornered physically. Silence seemed to be the only thing she could think of to protect herself.

'Very well,' he sighed, looking thoroughly sickened. 'I

can drive around for the rest of the day—all night if necessary. In the morning, if we're no further forward, I can phone Derrick Lean and tell him to destroy the shots. Following that, I can get in touch with all the photographers you work with and offer them more lucrative things, as well as more expensive and well known models. I assure you they'll be willing to drop you, no matter how friendly they appear to be now. Few photographers have the kind of name that Derrick Lean has, most of them are struggling to make ends meet. You can have a sharp and bitter lesson in life before the week is out.'

Merissa had already had a sharp and bitter lesson in life, did he but know it, and she knew perfectly well that what Julian Forrest said was true, the photographers were mainly struggling, as eager to find well paid work as she was herself. Every instinct, though, told her to fight him off—to invite him to do his worst. There was her mother, though, to say nothing of the debts, and it seemed that he had left her no hole to crawl into. Maybe if she explained . . . She glanced across at his unyielding face and decided against any explanation. He wouldn't believe it anyway, and if he did, he would probably simply shrug those great broad shoulders and point out that she was in an even bigger fix than he had imagined.

She told him the address defeatedly, her eyes on her clenched hands, and he said nothing at all but simply swung the car round and shot off at a speed that would probably have had her arrested if she had tried it in the Mini. Of course the poor old thing would have dropped to pieces first, she thought bitterly.

'God!' exclaimed Julian Forrest under his breath as he turned into her street, the sleek car moving along slowly, purring like an angry cat. It was the only word he had uttered since turning the car and heading for her home, and her face flushed at the sound of the appalled disgust in his voice.

At least her mother would be spared this embarrassment.

Tears suddenly glazed her eyes as she remembered the fleeting happiness she had felt as she had drifted between the tall columns of the centre, the lovely dress whispering around her ankles. It seemed to be burning a hole in her bag now, utterly out of place.

'Thanks for the lift, I'll be in touch about the job,' she said quickly, getting out as he opened the door and making rapidly for her own front door. Not rapidly enough. He was right beside her like a blue-eyed shadow as she reached her front doorstep.

'What do you want?' she asked sharply, looking up at him and forgetting for the moment that her eyes were rather dimmed with tears.

'I'm about to introduce myself to your mother,' he told her quietly, his eyes narrowing thoughtfully as he looked down at her. 'As your prospective fiancé I feel I should meet my future mother-in-law.'

'Look, you've got me trapped, I admit that,' Merissa said acidly, 'but there's no reason whatever why my mother should know about this. It's merely a job. She doesn't have to be pestered by everyone I work for.'

'But this job is different,' he said softly, watching her intently. 'It will take a considerable time and require a temporary new lifestyle. I think meeting her is a real necessity.'

'I haven't said yet that I'll take the job,' she reminded him, and his eyes hardened as he looked down at her.

'No, but you will. You have too much to lose, not to mention the money. I have you just where I want you, and I want the job done immediately. We'll discuss the finer points over dinner tonight,' he added, indicating the door, clearly tiring of being kept waiting.

'You'll not tell my mother about the engagement?' she asserted, giving him a hostile look, 'because if you intend to then the job's off, and you can do whatever you want to punish me!'

'Credit me with some sense, I have no intention of walking in now and frightening your mother to death,' he said irritably. 'I can tell you, though, that when the job begins, the engagement is real to everyone but our two selves—and that does include your mother. If word got out that it was a fake then there would be no use whatever in continuing, and I would really punish you then. When we've talked it through, your mother will be the first to know about it, and you will be deliriously happy.'

'You're joking, of course! I don't tell lies, especially to my mother!'

'You pretended a lie all the time you were being photographed today,' he reminded her testily. 'Extend your abilities a little. The job is going to pay well enough. She can laugh with you later. And, in case you think I'm joking, let me remind you that fiancées have certain duties that mothers might not approve of if they thought the whole thing was a lie.'

'What do you mean?' gasped Merissa, her face colouring.

'Not that again!' he rasped, glaring down at her. 'We've already been through that conversation, and I sincerely hope I'm not going to have to repeat everything I say to you. Once and for all, this is a business arrangement. I'll explain your duties later—now, do you mind?'

He obviously had no intention of going away and had clearly become extremely irritated by being kept on the doorstep, so Merissa hurriedly found her keys as several people stopped to stare at the car and the pair of them. They left precipitately after one glance from the cold brilliant eyes.

'Your car won't be there when you come out,' she muttered bitterly as she opened the front door.

'It will,' Julian assured her calmly. 'If anyone so much as trails a finger over it now that it's locked, all hell will break loose—you'll hear it.'

'I suppose it's wired to the police station too?' she queried spitefully.

'Not yet,' he murmured, giving her a little push forward and stepping after her into the little square hall. 'Maybe I'll get around to that when I've got you paid up and dispatched out of my life.'

'I've never wanted to be in your life,' she whispered angrily. 'I wish I'd never set eyes on you!'

'It wouldn't have made the slightest bit of difference,' he said in a low voice, his breath against her ear as he bent forward so that she could hear. 'I saw you, and that was all that was needed. Your fate was decided right then.'

Before she could answer, or even think about that remark, her mother appeared on the stairs and began to come unsteadily down.

'Merissa?' she sounded utterly breathless, and Merissa's heart sank. 'I'd no idea you'd be back so soon. I was resting. Oh . . .' She stopped suddenly as her eyes fell on the tall handsome man in the open doorway and colour flooded into her pale cheeks. For a minute she looked as if she was about to collapse and Merissa sprung forward, but she was not as fast as Julian Forrest. He was on the stairs almost before she had moved, his hand strong and steadying on her mother's arm.

'I'm sorry if my appearance startled you,' he said deeply and gently, his quiet concern leaving Merissa astonished. 'I've brought Merissa home. She's been working for me today and as we have a dinner date for tonight I had to find out where to pick her up. I'm sorry, we should have let you know.' He clearly meant that Merissa should have let her know, though how she could have been expected to do that when she was a captive in a fast car was beyond her. 'She finished early because she's very good at her job,' he added. 'I expect you already know that, though.'

'No—well, I've never seen her work, but she does most things very well,' her mother said proudly as he helped her down the stairs. 'You must be Mr Forrest, then. I knew she was working for you today at the new centre.'

They were quite clearly going to chat on happily, and Merissa watched numbly as they made their way down the stairs, her mother looking not nearly so shaky as she had done. They were beaming at each other, clearly taking a liking to each other on sight, and Merissa knew she wasn't included in Julian's warmth for one second; she was obviously at fault for not fighting her way out of a speeding car to telephone her mother and tell her she was bringing an arrogant lunatic home.

'Would you like a cup of tea?' Mrs Troy looked up at him with a coaxing smile, and he glanced at his watch and then grinned at her.

'If it's no trouble, I would. I've just had a very hectic and annoying bit of bargaining to do. I've got time for a quick cup of tea, though.' He never even glanced at Merissa, and just for once she could have given her mother a good shaking. Having Julian Forrest for tea was not her idea of paradise!

'Good, I'll get it now.' Her mother began to walk to the little kitchen, and he turned a baleful eye on Merissa, who still stood like stone with the door open.

'I wouldn't like to put you to any trouble,' he observed to her mother, but with his eyes on Merissa. 'As you're clearly not well, perhaps Merissa . . .'

'Oh, no, Mr Forrest!' Mrs Troy's voice brooked no argument. 'We have our little rituals and arrangements. Everything is ready. I get the tea. If it were left to Merissa I wouldn't be allowed to even move, and that's really bad for me. She cooks all the meals and she also works very hard. I get the tea!' She walked off into the kitchen, quite briskly as it turned out, and Merissa turned to close the door, her eyes angry and embarrassed.

'Come into my parlour,' she said, seething with anger as she turned back, the embarrassment hidden now. She showed Julian into the little sitting-room—and stopped in the doorway as his eyes moved over the really nice furnishings that they had managed to salvage from the wreck of their lives. He was looking around with open and cool assessment, and it drove her further on.

'It's quite safe to sit down,' she hissed angrily. 'Keep your fingers off the woodwork—those tables take a lot of polishing and I don't have all the time in the world.'

He sat in the biggest easy chair, his eyes intently on her.

He looked comfortable, at ease, and she was infuriated to think he was so self-assured and calm even in her own home, while she was hovering around in the doorway like an unwelcome visitor. She wasn't hovering for long, though, because he got up and came across to her, taking her arm and moving her to the settee.

'Come and sit down,' he said softly. 'You've been working and you've had a very unusual encounter with a very annoying man—me. Relax for a minute.'

She was sitting on the settee, Julian Forrest beside her, before she could protest, and she didn't have any further chance because her mother was there with a laden trolley, smiling all over her face.

'We hardly ever have visitors nowadays—well, only Hugh, really. It's lovely to have someone for tea. In the old days we always had visitors for tea. When Merissa's father was alive it was the . . .'

'I'll do the pouring if you like, Mummy,' Merissa interrupted quickly. 'I know Mr Forrest is really in a hurry.'

'Oh, all right, dear. I'll get the other cakes too, I think.' Mrs Troy hurried out, and Julian Forrest turned on Merissa like a panther, his eyes flashing sparks.

'Mr Forrest was a very big mistake, Merissa,' he warned softly. 'My name is Julian, and I know you're unhappy about this, but she's hardly likely to believe we're engaged if you call your future husband Mr Forrest.

'She'll never believe it anyway,' she answered stormily, trying to move away from the hard and powerful masculine body that was suddenly far too close.

'You can leave all that to me. Just don't sabotage the project before it's begun,' he threatened quietly, his eyes on her stubborn mouth. 'And don't look so angry and determined. You're sitting in your—parlour with the one you love, so get into the mood.'

'I'll never get into the mood,' she snapped in a little whisper, knowing that in this small house her mother would hear any moment. He had brought the battle right into her own home, and her annoyance and unease grew by the minute.

'You're too uptight, all wound up,' he murmured with irritating reasonableness. 'Come here.'

Before she could even utter the gasp of alarm that rose inside her, Julian's arm had moved from the back of the settee to encircle her shoulders and pull her close, and lips that were at once gentle and tempting brushed her hot cheeks, his free hand smoothing her hair away from her face.

'There,' he said quietly, as if she were a child on the edge of a tantrum, 'that's better, isn't it?'

All she could do was stare at him in utter astonishment, and it was all she could do to sit upright when her mother's steps came briskly back and he moved his arm to the back of the settee again.

'So what have you got on your books now that the centre is finished, Mr Forrest?' Mrs Troy asked pleasantly as they ate the tiny sandwiches and drank from her best china cups. She was really enjoying this, Merissa knew. It was so long since she had been able to entertain, as she had done so much when her father was alive.

'Well, we've usually got more work on than we can handle,' Julian said with a smile, playing the part of a visitor exactly as she knew her mother would have wished, just like the old days at the university when her father's students came. 'But the next thing I think I shall be personally involved with is something in Canada, although I haven't got the exact date yet.'

'Oh dear, you'll be all on edge, then, waiting,' smiled Mrs Troy, but he shook his head and looked mysterious.

'Ah, no! I have a very interesting and absorbing project going right this moment. That will keep me occupied nicely for a while and it's a challenge I have to take. I shall enjoy it, especially as I'm going to be the winner whatever happens.'

Merissa stiffened and made to move and get up, but the

hand behind her slid forward, well out of sight of her mother, and she felt the warm but warning fingers move under her hair and come to rest on the back of her neck, lingering there as if Julian hadn't quite made his mind up whether to take her neck in a steel-like grip or not. She sat back, listening to her mother's happy chatter, and presently the fingers moved to stroke her neck, moving up under her hair to the tight muscles that were threatening to give her a king-sized headache.

She dared not move. Julian was capable of almost anything, and she was in no doubt that he would announce the engagement there and then if she annoyed him enough. Her mother seemed in blissful ignorance of any undercurrents. She was dispensing tea, all her past habits surfacing, her charm at its fullest flow, and Merissa bit her lip and stuck it out rather than subject her to any shock.

His fingers were making her legs weak, making every part of her relaxed and warm, and she struggled to keep him from knowing exactly what was happening inside her, but unknowingly her tight hands relaxed too and lay almost languidly on her lap, and he certainly didn't miss that, because as she glanced sidelong at him his eyes were on her hands before lifting with amused triumph to meet her own appalled and darkening eyes.

It was a relief when he finally stood and announced that he really must go as he had several things to do before he collected Merissa for dinner, and Merissa stood quickly on legs that trembled slightly, anxious to get him off the premises with all speed.

She trailed behind him to the hall as her mother began to gather the remains of the small but successful tea-party together.

'I'll pick you up at seven,' he said shortly, looking as if he was about to walk off without another word.

'What shall I wear?' she asked a trifle anxiously, already feeling subdued and beaten by his onslaught on her. She wasn't up to further battle at the moment.

'As we have plenty to discuss, we'll eat in a quiet place,' Julian said without even glancing at her. 'Something subdued, please, and the normal hairdo will be quite adequate. We don't want to look as if we're on our way to a witches' convention.' He simply walked out, and she had great pleasure in slamming the door after him, only to have to open it a few minutes later as he rang the bell.

'Your bag,' he murmured in an amused voice, holding out the bag she carried her equipment in, a bag she had forgotten completely when she had tried to make a quick escape so pointlessly. 'I do hope the money isn't in here,' he added softly, clearly not wanting her mother to hear. 'I know you haven't had time to spend it. Luckily the car was locked.'

'Just go!' Merissa burst out angrily. 'I'll be ready at seven, and until then I'll be able to imagine you don't exist!'

'Ah, your attitude is going to have to change,' he warned in a taunting voice. 'I'll have to give you a few lessons in how to be an adoring fiancée, otherwise nobody is going to believe it at all.' His eyes locked with her dark angry ones, and although he taunted she could see an anger deep inside him that was being held in check by a supreme will that was frightening.

'The impossibility of that is so obvious that I can't think why you still want me for the job!' she retorted with a withering look.

'I want you because you're perfect,' he assured her quietly. 'And don't go imagining I'll let you off the hook. Don't be fooled by my attitude towards your mother. As far as you're concerned there's not one soft spot in me.'

He turned and went to his car, and Merissa felt her anger drain away as she watched his tall figure slide into the driving seat and saw the capable hands come to the wheel. Why did he dislike her so much? She didn't care, of course, but it was still a puzzle, and deep down she knew it was beginning to hurt.

CHAPTER THREE

JULIAN FORREST's idea of not being late seemed to be to arrive half an hour early, because Merissa heard the doorbell at six-thirty and his deep voice in the hall as her mother let him in. He sounded warm and friendly, none of the harsh edge to his voice that was there more often than not when he spoke to her. Let him wait, she thought bitterly as her mother took him into the neat little sitting-room. She could hear them chatting away like old friends as she put the finishing touches to her make-up.

She had decided to do her hair in exactly the same way that she had worn it for the afternoon's photographic session, demurely and elegantly, and she had also decided to wear a very demure dress that covered her in almost every place, but as she heard the murmur of polite and friendly talk from the room immediately below her bedroom she found her temper rising. Julian wasn't an ogre, then, except with her!

She looked at the pleasant, quiet dress and then firmly placed it back on the hanger, choosing instead a jumpsuit that looked very much like a tigerskin. It was something that she never wore; it had been bought for a job she had done the year before and it was far too eye-catching to wear outside the studio. Well, it was too eye-catching for her to wear anyway. It was tight at the ankles, fitting closely to her curves, the neck a deep V in front, and she finished it off with a thin gold belt before slipping on high-heeled mules also in gold. Dangling golden earrings finished off the effect, and she applied plenty of gloss to her mouth over a pale lipstick that stood out against the tan of her face.

Satisfied, she stood in front of the mirror, hands on her hips, and studied the effect. Julian wanted a model? He had one! No longer herself but a glittering vision that seemed to have stepped straight from the cover of an expensive magazine, Merissa walked downstairs, a gold evening bag in her hand as she met her mother in the hall.

'Oh! You're ready, Merissa?' Her mother sounded just a little disappointed. 'You look lovely,' she added doubtfully. Merissa smiled and kissed her cheek. She knew all too well that her mother didn't like to think too deeply of her modelling work. To Mrs Troy the cloistered life of a university was the only life to live, and she felt that Merissa was always at risk. She had no idea how much more at risk she was now with this sensuous and powerful man.

'Thank you, Mummy. Don't bother with tea, if that's where you were going. We'll be off now.'

She wanted him out of the house as quickly as possible and away from her mother. Heaven only knew what he had been saying to her. If he had even hinted at this ridiculous engagement ... Merissa walked into the sitting-room, making the sort of entrance that her training had perfected, and then stopped very abruptly as she realised her mistake in issuing any kind of challenge to a man like this.

His eyes moved deliberately over her, lingering on the swell of her breasts before moving downwards to inspect every curve of her body, and she felt a flush of colour that started in her throat and deepened until it seemed to be covering every part of her. There was no smile in his eyes as they raised to hers and none of the compliment that she was used to when a man inspected her appearance. Julian knew what she had done deliberately. He was quite aware of her defiant actions upstairs, and for a stinging moment she wondered if he was about to order her back to change into something more suitable, but clearly he was not. His eyes fell again to her throat and moved back to the rise of her breasts that seemed to fascinate him.

'I hope this will do?' she said with as much defiance as her quickened breathing would allow.

'Do for what?' he queried, his eyes never rising from their intent scrutiny of her.

'You—you did say we were going somewhere quiet,' she

stammered, almost ready to back out and make a run for it.

'Quiet? Yes,' he murmured, his gaze coming back at last to hers and holding her defiant dark eyes for a second. 'Let's go!' Suddenly he seemed angry, and she was glad about that but oddly shaken, greatly pleased to hear her mother's voice as she walked out of the room to find her just coming into the hall.

'Don't wait up for me,' she warned, giving her a quick kiss on the cheek.

'I won't, dear. I know you'll be quite safe with Mr Forrest.'

Merissa nearly shrieked hysterically. Safe? He was the nearest thing to a big prowling jungle cat she had ever seen, and she had played right into his hands with her provocative outfit. She was never going to be safe with him, and she hoped something would come up over this outing to make him decide she was really most unsuitable. Perhaps if she behaved in a flashy and sensuous manner he would make his mind up that she was not after all suitable to be introduced into his world as anything at all, least of all a fiancée.

He said nothing until they had pulled away from the house, and then his brilliant gaze moved quickly over her.

'Trying to tempt me?' he enquired softly, his eyes firmly on the road as she glanced angrily across at him. There was nothing but sardonic amusement on his face when she stared at his hard profile.

'I don't waste my time on impossibilities,' she snapped. 'We're going to thrash out an absurd business arrangement, and in any case, one doesn't tempt a rattlesnake, one takes a stick and . . .'

To her annoyance Julian threw his head back and laughed.

'Oddly enough, although I realise all too well what the significance is of that particular outfit; you look quite beautiful. Every inch the successful and high-class model. You were made to order, Merissa sweetheart.'

'What—what did you call me?' she gasped, swinging startled eyes to his lean dark face.

'Practising,' he informed her, a smile tugging at the corner of his well shaped mouth. 'Just practising. Seeing how it rolls off the tongue. I think I'll be able to manage it. After all, in public we really will have to act the part—you know that. Want to give it a try yourself?'

'I'll tackle the nasty bits when I have to and not before!' she snapped, glad of the darkness to hide her blushes. 'I know all the necessary words.'

'Naturally. I imagine you've had plenty of practice—foolish of me to think you'd need a rehearsal,' he remarked scathingly. 'I quite forgot about Goddard for a moment. Just pretend I'm him, when the time comes, although of course you won't be expected to go quite that far with me. The odd adoring look will do.'

He relapsed into angry silence, and Merissa let him. After all, this was his idea, and if he imagined there was an impatient lover waiting in the wings then so much the better. Clearly he was going to use any kind of tactic that came into his head, like his tactics on the settee this afternoon for example. She wished she hadn't thought of that, because her whole body seemed to remember, not just her outraged mind, and it brought to her with an uncomfortable suddenness the fact that she was sitting next to a very virile male animal, one who was dangerous and utterly unsympathetic towards her. She clenched her hands on her bag and kept silent also.

'Maybe, as this is the first time we'll be seen together in public,' said Julian quietly after a while, 'we'd better start being a little more friendly. Just sit a little less stiffly and think nice thoughts. It will do until I've got you trained.'

'You'll never . . .' she began angrily, but he let her go no further.

'Oh, but I will, Merissa,' he said softly. 'You'll earn every penny of the money you're going to get, and you'll leave my life a greatly subdued person. Goddard will hardly know you!'

'Don't bank on it!' she said bitingly. 'Certainly don't hold your breath!'

'Would you like to bet the fifteen thousand?' he tempted. 'Double or nothing?'

'I don't gamble!' Merissa snapped.

'You have a virtue?' he asked with exaggerated surprise. 'My mind refuses to absorb it. Leave it with me, will you? I'll ponder on it a while.'

Merissa closed her mouth firmly. There was no point in trying to get the better of him like this. She needed to secure her shell, and she had no further patience for verbal acrobatics.

The lights in the restaurant were not so subdued after all, and she felt every eye on them as they followed the waiter to their table in the corner. Of course, Julian Forrest was a man to draw the eye. His mid-grey suit fitted him perfectly, his hair was well groomed, his handsome face very masculine and striking. He was more than a little daunting, so assured and successful, with an animal grace that had every female head turning to look with speculation as he passed. Merissa tried hard to feel nothing, but her old shyness reared its head and she had to act her part very hard indeed to prevent herself from turning and dashing for the door. She knew of course that she looked good, in a rather glossy way. She knew too that as the women were looking Julian over there was also plenty of male eyes on her, but as usual it gave her no satisfaction.

She was very glad of the hand under her arm as Julian ushered her across the floor, and she glanced up at him from beneath her thick lashes to see a small but definite smile hovering on the sensuous mouth. She could only think he noticed her discomfort and was amused by it. There was definitely a streak of cruelty in him. She imagined the watching women noticed that too. Maybe it excited them.

'What would you like, Merissa?' he asked, pleasantly solicitous as the waiter hovered over them.

'Er—you choose for me, please,' she answered quietly. 'I've never been here before.'

He shot her a quick keen glance and then ordered for both of them, while Merissa sat very still, looking at her clenched hands as they lay in her lap. Her act was slipping, she thought wildly. Inside she was in a turmoil. If only the lights were lower, if only she had worn the nice drab dress. She had wilfully placed herself in this situation where every eye seemed to be on her. She told herself forcefully that to imagine everyone was looking at you was a conceit, they were most definitely not, but a quick glance round assured her that they were—at least they were looking at her table, maybe at Julian. It didn't really matter. She would rather have had her food passed to her under the table.

'What's wrong?' he asked softly as the waiter left. 'Are you all right?'

'Perfectly!' Merissa answered more sharply than she intended and for a short while he was quiet, clearly annoyed that his considerate remark had met with such a sharp reply.

'Out of your depth?' he asked after a while, no concern in his voice now. It nearly had the effect that he did not want at all. She nearly burst into tears. It really had been a rotten day, what with one thing and another. There had been more bills in the mail too when she had got to them after he had left the little tea-party.

'Why don't you just leave me alone?' she whispered shakily.

'I can't, Merissa. I can't.' He said it with an odd inflection that had her looking up into his eyes, to find them soft and smiling, sympathetic. 'In many ways you're a fraud, aren't you?' he asked in that smoky voice. 'You're all nerves. It took more courage than I realised for you to go out on to that catwalk. You hide in a studio, don't you?'

She stared back at him before dropping her eyes, her cheeks flushed with embarrassment and anxiety. He was enough trouble without this apparent capacity to read her character. Not all of it, she thought bitterly; according to him she was nothing much.

'I've just had a bad day, as you can imagine, you having been the cause of it,' she answered with a touch of annoyance to cover her anxiety. 'Now I'm to be some sort of a human sacrifice!'

'It really doesn't need to be like that,' he assured her, still apparently hanging on to his considerable temper. 'It could be quite a bit of fun, if you'd let it be that. The pay is good, the working conditions will be little short of luxurious. Nothing will be expected of you that you're not more than capable of producing.'

'Except that I'm not doing it of my own free will. I've been tricked and bullied into it. Threatened and—and kidnapped!'

'Kidnapped?' Julian laughed softly and to her consternation, one strong hand came out to cover her own slim fingers. 'How do you make out that you were kidnapped when all I did was take you home? I even stayed for tea, and thoroughly enjoyed myself.'

'Well, I didn't enjoy myself!' Merissa looked up at him in anoyance, quite forgetting now to be nervous in this place, the people here disappearing from her mind.

'Oh? I thought for a few moments there that you were really enjoying it,' he said softly, the blue eyes intent on her face. 'Actually I was waiting for you to leap away from my hand, but you never did. Finally I thought I'd better get out of there before you started to purr quietly. Your mother would never have understood.'

She snatched her hand away and glared at him. He really had helped her into her shell, and she was so intent on battling with him that people could have come to stand round the table and take notes for all she cared.

'Look, don't bother to try and soften me up!' she snapped. 'You've already walked into my life uninvited and laid down the law. At the moment I can see no other course but to agree to your impossible suggestion, but I certainly don't have to like it and it will definitely not be fun for me. I'll see to it that it's not fun for you either. I intend to be a very big business worry!'

'If you like,' Julian growled in annoyance, leaning back again, well away from her. 'I'll explain as we eat and then you can weigh up your chances of survival. But understand this—I meant every word I said when I threatened to tear up today's shots and warn off Derrick Lean and the others. Walk out in the middle of this meal and you're finished as a photographic model. The best thing you'll get will be work like the promotion at Fitzpatrick's, a chance to perform athletically and show off your flimsies!'

'I was tripped!' she snapped, her colour flaring into her face, and he nodded, his eyes watching her blushes.

'I know,' he said more quietly. 'I saw the whole thing, and I admire courage and quick thinking. I suppose I decided right then that you were the person I wanted if you could act the part.'

'You'd seen me before and already decided on my character,' Merissa accused angrily. 'Don't pretend it was the first time you'd set eyes on me. You thought you had the right to speak to me in any way you chose from the moment you saw me. You decided on sight that I was—was no better than I should be!'

'Are you, sweetheart?' Julian enquired scathingly as the waiter arrived and put all conversation at an end. She was glad of the respite, because she was unaccountably on the edge of tears, and he was not the sort of man to either offer a shoulder to cry on or to back down and release her from this monstrous arrangement. He simply intended to make her life harder than it was already, and she wondered how long she could keep up this pretence.

'Let's get down to business,' he said in a hard voice as they began to eat. 'That's the only reason why we're here, and as you so obviously like this as little as I do we may as well cut out the chatter and begin. You can make your comments when I've finished.'

She didn't bother to answer, and he began at once as she kept her eyes firmly on her plate.

'There are one or two ladies who are cluttering up my life,' he confessed. 'One in particular—Felicity. She has the mad idea that I intend to marry her, and she couldn't be more wrong. Unfortunately my parents like her enormously, and I'm very fond of my parents. So, I intend to become safely and securely engaged to someone who's doing it merely as a job and over whom I have considerable control—you! When the lady has taken the message completely to heart, the engagement will be at an end and our paths need never cross again. You will by then have the security of a considerable sum of money and the chance to work with the best people. I'll be going overseas to work for a while in any case, so we'll both be out of the limelight and out from under each other's feet. Anyone else with the same aspirations can meanwhile be skittled by the same ball.'

He paused, but Merissa said nothing, beginning to be alarmed by his cold-blooded frankness. He was right, she was out of her depth. She stole a curious glance at him and as quickly looked away when she saw the odd look he was giving her. She felt like some small, furry creature who had inadvertently poked its head out of a hole to look at the weather and found a hard-eyed fox waiting to have a hearty lunch.

'These people are impossible to avoid,' he continued after an uneasy pause, while Merissa tried to gather her breath and slow down the suddenly unsteady beating of her heart. 'They move in my circle, dine where I dine. They will be the ones you have to put down—hence the ladylike requirements. They would hardly take you seriously if you appeared looking as you looked at the promotion.'

'You know damned well I had to be dressed like that!' she snapped angrily. 'You've seen me before and you know the promotion was as much a fancy dress thing as any Hallowe'en party! And why me?' she added, looking up at him as anger stifled the hurt that flooded inside her. 'Why not a really nice girl?'

'Because the ladies of my acquaintance can play really rough,' he informed her smoothly. 'A really nice girl, as you put it, would be demolished first time out. You can take care of yourself and you can act the part.'

'What makes you think I can take care of myself?' Merissa asked curiously. Every time he had seen her she had been in a panic, simply because he had looked at her.

'I'm not altogether dumb,' he rejoined shortly. 'I saw you

with Goddard, for one thing, and that alone is enough to make me sure you're not one hundred per cent innocent. Apart from that I know these promotions—God, I've been invited to plenty, and there are some that purely in the line of business I can't get out of. Nobody acts like that girl did on the catwalk unless they've been provoked to the point of rage. She doesn't have either your figure or your looks, so I would imagine she's stuck with that kind of job, and Clare Anders doesn't look to me like any easy touch. The other girl risked her place at the agency to get even with you, so you must have provoked her to the limit. Even then, you got the better of her and gained all the applause, while she's probably been given the sack.'

'You have no idea what goes on in the dressing-rooms,' she accused quietly. 'If I couldn't defend myself I might as well pack it up and sit at home crying.'

'Definitely not your scene,' he said with laughter in his voice,' and you're only saying what I've already said. Obviously you can take care of yourself, hence the choice. You're beautiful enough to make it a feasible idea that I should have chosen you, you can act like a charming and shy lady and you have steel inside you, just below the skin. As I said, you're perfect for me.'

What was the use? Everything she said merely put her more deeply into the pit.

'Your mother has asthma, doesn't she?' he asked, changing direction with bewildering speed and not at all put out that Merissa merely sat quiet and sombre.

'Yes.' Brevity seemed to be a good idea. The less he knew about anything the better. She was giving no information to the enemy.

'Yet you allow her to live in that place, with all the money you earn? According to Mrs Anders, you're always working and trying to get more work all the time. Can't you do without a few expensive clothes and rent somewhere better for her?'

'Can't you mind your own business?' she asked tightly.

'This has nothing whatever to do with you and your wretched job!'

'The expensive flimsies are more important than your mother's health?' Julian slated quietly. 'Those you wore in the dressing-room last week must have cost a fortune.'

'Will you please drop the subject?' she asked crossly, blushing to the roots of her hair. 'What I wear under—underneath has nothing whatever to do with you!'

'It lingers in my mind,' he said softly, sitting back and watching her flushed face. 'I'm really surprised that it bothers you. They were a present from an admirer?'

'They were a bonus,' she snapped, 'from an advertisement I did. Now get off the subject!'

'And the beautiful tan?' he goaded. 'Was that a bonus too, or did you go off for a quiet week in the South of France while your mother held the pitiful fort?'

'Yes,' she lied glibly. 'Frenchmen are so sexy.'

'Which brings me to a point!' said Julian, suddenly savage. 'While you're acting your part as my fiancée, there'll be no men!'

'Not even a teensy-weensy little one?' taunted Merissa, searching through her mind for the last time anyone had kissed her, apart from the rather fatherly kisses that Hugh bestowed on her from time to time as he left her at her door. She could only recall a boy at university—yes, that was it, she had been far too busy struggling with debts and worries since then. If Hugh had not continued to come to see them and had not occasionally taken her out there would have been no outings at all.

'Don't try my patience, Merissa!' Julian ground out. 'No men! The deal's off if I see you so much as glance sideways at one, and then, of course, reprisals take place.'

She glared at him, but his blue-eyed stare won and she dropped her eyes.

'Very well,' she agreed, managing a sigh which infuriated him into silence for a while. He spoke when he had controlled his obvious temper.

'Since meeting your mother, I've decided to add a bonus to the job.'

'A bonus!' Merissa's head shot up as her mind knocked off a few more debts.

'Not cash, my greedy little beauty,' he told her with satisfaction. 'The bonus is for your mother.'

He signalled the waiter and paid the bill, helping her to her feet to escort her from the restaurant, and by now she was too puzzled to be nervous.

'Ah!' The hand on her arm tightened as they crossed the room and he pulled her close to his side. 'Sharpen your wits! You're on duty sooner than I expected.'

For a second she hadn't the faintest idea what he was talking about, but that soon resolved itself as they drew level with a table where four people were dining, and one of them stretched out a slender arm bedecked with gold bangles to arrest Julian in his path.

'Julian darling!' The husky voice was far more penetrating than Merissa would have liked, because all eyes turned on them and her nerves threatened to swamp her again instantly. 'I saw you come in, but you never gave me even the tiniest little glance. I would have come over to you, but I could see you were having sharp words with your—date.' The last word was almost a question, and although she was addressing her words to Julian, the sharp eyes were on Merissa.

'Louise!' Julian's voice held a beautifully combined mixture of surprise and indifference, all overlaid with a cool politeness. 'Quarrelling? No, we were definitely not quarrelling, were we, Merissa?'

'Er—no, a slight difference of opinion, that's all.' Merissa was utterly in the dark. The encounter had been so unexpected that there had been no time for any briefing, and she knew she was expected to play this by ear. A lovely opportunity to drop him in the soup and put an end to this farce, but even as she thought it Julian's eyes turned on her with a smiling warning as his grip tightened. Reprisals! She could almost read the word on his face, and she decided to play the game to the best of her ability.

'Oh, I'm sorry, sweetheart,' he murmured, seeing her capitulation and relaxing his angry grip on her. 'This is Louise Atherton. I forgot for the moment that you haven't yet met all my acquaintances. Louise, Merissa Troy.'

Being classified as an acquaintance was definitely a put-down for the hard-eyed woman who gazed up at them, and her eyes narrowed angrily too at the smoothness of the endearment that Julian had used to Merissa. She kept the smile on her face, though, and leaned back provocatively, her green eyes on Merissa.

In her way, she was quite beautiful, Merissa noted. She had red hair, short and beautifully styled, and she had money, there was little doubt of that. Her dress was not to Merissa's taste, but it was expensive, wickedly so in her opinion. If this was the sort of person that Julian wanted to get rid of then she had her work cut out. He clearly had no idea that she was incapable of the kind of in-fighting that would be necessary. Here was someone intelligent and beautiful, backed by wealth and accustomed to having her own way with everything.

'Well, Miss Troy, you seem to have come off fairly well after a difference of opinion with Julian. You often reduce me to tears, don't you, Julian darling?'

'Oh, what a shame!' said Merissa, looking up with a sweetly shocked face at Julian. 'I didn't know you could be cruel, Julian. I hope you're not going to be cruel to me—I just couldn't bear it.'

'Now how could anyone be cruel to you, my sweet?' he drawled, delighted laughter in his eyes as he gazed down at her. Obviously she had struck just the right note. She had done it instinctively, knowing it was not in her to keep up any kind of bitterness for long. If Julian wanted this game played then he was going to have to be the one to do the fighting; she would have to be the pawn in the game and trust to him to protect her. He seemed to be reading her thoughts again, because his arm slid round her and he pulled her close.

'I couldn't say one harsh word to you, you're too gentle and vulnerable. My only instinct is to protect you.'

'How lovely to hear a man talk like that,' one of the other women at the table put in softly, and Louise Atherton gave a trill of harsh laughter, her eyes hard and green on Merissa.

'And how unlike Julian,' she murmured. 'I wonder what he's after?'

Merissa's blush was perfect. It came without any warning at the suggestive tone, but it couldn't have been done better if she had planned it.

'Louise!' one of the men grated in shocked and embarrassed tones, clearly feeling protective himself, and it gave Julian the chance he had been waiting for.

'She knows what I want, that's what the difference of opinion was,' he said quietly. 'However, I've won, so there's no need to worry about us, Louise. We're getting engaged now instead of later in the month. Now I really must get Merissa home, she's not used to this night life and I don't want to wear her out.'

He nodded pleasantly and ushered Merissa out, his arm still around her, and she glanced at Louise as they passed. The brilliant smile was still in place, but under her make-up she was white and drawn.

'Why did you do that?' Merissa snapped as they walked out into the cool night air. 'You dropped that bombshell without any kind of consultation with me. I'm in this too, you know!'

'In at the deep end now,' he observed with satisfaction. 'It's as good a way to begin as any.'

'I've never said I'd do this—this job!' she reminded him angrily.

'No, not in so many words, but we both know you will, especially when I tell you about the bonus. You'll have even more to lose if you back out now. In any case, Louise, as you probably realise, is one of the people I want off my back. Surely you didn't take to her?'

'Is it likely?' she asked scathingly as he helped her into

the car. 'She's really poisonous!'

'Well we've established our tactics,' he shrugged comfortably as he got in beside her and started the engine, pulling smoothly and quietly out into the traffic. 'You're a darling that I need to protect, and as you appear to be able to blush and looked shocked and utterly defenceless to order, it looks to me as if it will work very well indeed.'

Merissa was sure it would because all she would have to do was be herself. It was fine, providing that Julian would always be there to step in with anything nasty, and providing too that she could survive the necessary close contact with this unpredictable man. She disliked him very much, she was certain of that, but she knew also she was not immune to his magnetism, to the overwhelming aura of sexuality that seemed to be as much a part of him as his keen and intelligent mind and his hard determination to get the better of any and everybody.

'You'd better explain the bonus,' she said quietly, not wishing to discuss further her ability to blush and look vulnerable. To her it was no asset, especially with him.

'Yes,' he said evenly. 'I have a country cottage. It's not too far from London, but the air is good and it comes complete with housekeeper, a comfortable little woman by the name of Mrs Boddy. She lives in, so there'd be no need to worry. I intend to let your mother have the cottage and she can move her treasured possessions there, moving out anything she doesn't need from the place. When the job is finished to my satisfaction,' he added finally, 'I'll give her the deeds and the cottage will be hers permanently.'

Merissa stared at him in the lights of the passing cars, utterly bewildered.

'Why—why are you doing this?' she blurted out. 'Why? You know I can't refuse your job. You've got me in a corner. Why this generosity?'

'I like her,' said Julian with an offhand shrug of his shoulders.

'She won't take it!' Merissa said with certainty.

'She will,' he countered with equal certainty. 'She'll

believe I'm your real fiancé, her future son-in-law. All the more reason why she shouldn't know the truth until later—leave her to me.'

She was silent for a minute, digesting this, realising that with everything he did she was becoming more deeply embroiled in his life, an anxiety growing deep inside her that was stilling her tongue more and more.

'How can I get from there to my job?' she asked worriedly. 'How often will you expect to see me?'

'I'll expect to see you every time I turn my head,' he told her quietly. 'You won't need to travel. You're going to live with me.'

'You,' said Merissa, her face hot in the darkness, 'are out of your mind! Forget the whole thing!'

'You prefer Goddard, or the sexy Frenchman?' he enquired scathingly. 'Believe me, Miss Troy, Goddard will find you exactly as he left you, although more subdued. You will live in my house on the outskirts of London. Your chaperon is a lady who keeps house for me and who will sleep on a mat outside your bedroom door if your unbelievably virtuous mind requires it.'

She simply sat stunned, unable to think of a thing to say, although the flush refused to leave her face and her mind was darting frantically this way and that to find some escape.

'Here we are,' he said quietly as they pulled up in front of her house and stopped in the darkened street,' back to Hell's Corner. The sooner we get your mother away from here, the better. We'll go in and announce our engagement right now, then we can get moving on that particular project.'

'I—I can't! I—I'm not ready!' she cried, in a panic now that the moment of decision had arrived, forced on her so suddenly and unexpectedly.

'You need to change into something more suitable for lying?' he asked scathingly. 'Come on, Merissa! You probably spend half your life lying to her. She's not the sort of mother who smiles benignly on the sort of antics you undoubtedly get up to.'

'I don't lie to her! I can't!' Merissa exclaimed in despair. 'I know it will be better for her to move and I really will tell her, but I can't just walk in and do it cold, like that. I've never lied to her before.'

Julian looked at her strangely for a long time until she dropped her eyes and looked fixedly at her shaking hands.

'All right,' he said softly. 'So we've discovered another virtue, you don't lie to your mother. This time, though, you've got to, for her sake, and if you can't do it cold, we'll have to get you into a convincing mood. I don't want her refusing the cottage.'

He reached out for her, his hands on her shoulders and then sliding down her back to her waist, pulling her close, and she went as stiff as a startled cat.

'What—what are you doing?' she gasped in a frightened little voice.

'I'm putting some colour into your act,' he murmured, drawing her across the seat and completely into his arms. 'A few stars in your eyes and she'll swallow it all in one go. I don't want you going in there looking so desperate and shaky.'

'No!' She struggled as it all dawned on her, but it was too late, he had her fast against the hard power of his body, his lips brushing her gently, his hands sure and firm on her back and waist.

'Calm down,' he murmured softly against her lips. 'It really isn't going to hurt in the least, and this startled virgin act is altogether too much. Relax.'

No virgin had ever been quite so startled, Merissa thought frantically, but there was no escaping the seductively moving hands or the hard firm lips that swooped down on hers.

For a second she tossed her head, struggling, but then a wonderful warmth flooded through her, irresistible and unexpected, making all her limbs relax, and she felt the tempo of his kiss change as if this too was a shock to him.

The pressure of his mouth increased as his hand moved to tangle in her hair, his other hand to slide to her hips, pulling her even closer, and he persisted until her mouth opened beneath his, allowing him to invade the sweetness of her mouth.

Excitement grew inside her as his hand moved slowly over her with a sensuous pleasure that brought a low moan from her lips.

'It's all right, Merissa,' he said against the soft skin of her throat, his voice deep and thick. 'Relax. Enjoy it.' She couldn't help but relax and enjoy it, because he was far too experienced for her, playing on her feelings like a master musician on a violin until her whole body was alive with pleasure.

Panic gripped her when his fingers found her breast and gently moved against it, sending shudders of delight through her, but he stifled her little gasp of alarm with warm, gentle lips. His hand slid inside the deep V of her neckline and found the warmth of her breast, caressing it with a strange tenderness that left her helpless and shaking, his fingers unerringly finding the hard, tightly budded centre and coaxing it to stinging life.

'Julian! No!' It was a pitiful attempt at refusal and quite lost on him, because he seemed to have forgotten the purpose of the exercise. He was utterly given up to the pleasure and sensuality of his own actions, and Merissa knew she was powerless to stop him.

'You're as soft as a kitten in my arms,' he breathed huskily. 'Pliant and willing. A sexy little kitten.'

His mouth swooped back to hers, kissing her deeply, and she mindlessly wound her arms around his neck, responding unthinkingly, instinctively until they were pressed together, straining to get even closer.

It was Julian who pulled away, his breathing harsh, his hands still holding her fiercely to him as he stared down into her eyes.

'My God!' he breathed. 'You're as sensuous as a cat, all eager response. What have we here, my little fighting lady? I don't think you're going to have any difficulty in pretending any engagement. I only hope I'll survive without having my mind bent. A man could go mad with you in his arms!'

She pulled away and he let her go with obvious reluctance, his harsh, intent gaze making her flush even more.

'You said I had to play a part,' she whispered shakily, by no means in control of her feelings and wondering what had happened to her there. Even now she wanted to be back in his arms, feeling those lips over hers. 'I—I can act really well.'

'That was no act!' he ground out roughly. 'And if it was, then it was a very dangerous act with a very obvious ending—but then I expect that you know that, having so clearly been there before.'

Julian seemed furious now and she felt too shaken to protest. What did it matter what he thought of her? This was only a job anyway, and after that she would never see him again.

'I know when to stop,' she said in a brittle voice, feeling ready to break into pieces.

'I'm glad to hear it,' he rasped, 'because I've just discovered that I don't. One of us will have to be in control. Dare I leave it to you?'

'Please!' She looked up at him miserably, hurt by the constant blows to her self-esteem, and he pulled her back into his arms, looking down at her intently.

'Please what?' he asked tightly. 'Please let me go home, or please do it all again?' She shook her head miserably, tears already on the way, and Julian suddenly kissed her trembling mouth hard and fast, his hands cupping her face.

'OK, little fraud,' he murmured. 'Let's go and see your mother.'

Her mother was shocked and, left to herself, Merissa knew she would never have managed it, but Julian was apparently capable of anything, and although he had confessed a liking for her mother to the extent that he was prepared to put his cottage at her disposal, even to give it to her when the job was finished, he had no hesitation whatever in lying to her. His manner was easy and bland, so much so that Merissa began to suspect that lies sprang readily from him at most times. 'You never mentioned it, Merissa,' her mother said, looking very hurt that she should not have known about this most important event in her daughter's life.

'I only asked her this evening,' Julian confessed smoothly, his arm tightening around Merissa—to add colour to things, Merissa thought shakily.

'Even so, you hardly know each other,' her mother continued stubbornly, looking more alive and alert than she had done for a long time now.

'Does that matter so very much?' Julian asked softly. 'We'll get to know each other a good deal more while we're engaged. It's not as if we intend to rush off out and marry at once, there's plenty of time before we do that.'

Like the rest of our lives, Merissa thought thankfully. It seemed to be a dialogue between her mother and Julian, giving her the strangest feeling that it did not really concern her at all.

To be quite truthful with herself, she had only had a very slight grip on reality since his kisses in the car, and his arm around her waist was not helping at all. It wasn't allowing her to come down to earth because it was not by any means an indifferent grip. His arm was warm and firm, his fingers splayed out over her hip with a coaxing pressure that refused to be ignored. If he thought this was helping then he was very much mistaken.

'Well—if you're both sure ...' Mrs Troy said finally, looking at Merissa a little worriedly.

'We are.' Julian spoke for her, his free hand tilting her face, allowing him to look into her eyes. 'Aren't we, darling?' Her mother was just a little too close for the threat Merissa knew he intended to be allowed to show in his eyes. They were as blue as a summer sky, she thought dazedly as she simply gazed back at him. She had never seen eyes so brilliantly blue that she simply wanted to go on looking into them.

'Come back down to earth,' Julian said softly with all the intimacy of a real fiancé in his tone, and she blushed painfully at the really expert tenderness in his voice, her attitude finally convincing her mother.

'Well, in that case,' she said with a sudden spark of real life, 'I'm dying to see the ring.'

'Tomorrow,' said Julian in an almost faraway voice, still gazing into Merissa's face. 'Tomorrow we get the ring and we all go out to celebrate —we'll have a real engagement party during next week.'

The announcement snapped Merissa out of her daze. Was there really anything at all that he had not covered with some plan? She could see that tomorrow he would want to coax her mother into the idea of the cottage, but what was the purpose of an engagement party?

CHAPTER FOUR

HE told her as she was dutifully showing him to the door. He took her hand and drew her out into the relative privacy of the darkened street at her whispered question.

'Naturally we need an engagement party,' he said testily as if she was the world's most successful moron. 'How do we manage to spread the news quickly around my circle without one?'

'You could let them find out ...' Merissa began, her words dying away at the irritated look in his eyes.

'I want them off my back immediately, like yesterday!' he snapped. 'Felicity is going to take a little longer as my parents are involved, but Louise can be dispatched really quickly.'

'You're really cold-blooded, aren't you?' she asked with feeling. 'Hasn't it occurred to you that it may really be a blow to at least one of them? If one of them really loves you . . .'

'You think it possible?' Julian asked wryly, his head sideways as he gave her a narrow-eyed look that seemed to be very piercing in the dingy glow of the street lighting. 'How could anyone love a cold-blooded and cruel person like me? They couldn't possibly. Surely you above all must realise that.'

'May-maybe they don't realise just what you're like,' she stammered, her heart accelerating frighteningly at his intent looks. 'After all, you have my mother eating out of your hand.'

'But of course, you know exactly what I'm like,' he told her softly. 'Don't forget, though, that you're being paid most generously to be on my side. I haven't either lost sight of the fact that after setting you on as an attacking and destructive force that would sweep everyone in my path aside with an efficient and ruthless speed, I find I'm the one to have to be ruthless, you being too tender and timid to do more than blush and shiver.'

'Then I'm not really suitable, am I?' she got in quickly. 'You made a mistake. We can tell my mother the whole story now and just forget the whole thing.'

She looked up hopefully to find him laughing quietly, not one bit put out by her logic, and she jumped nervously when his arms came round her.

'Already the game is under way,' he reminded her. 'Louise has been told. You imagine I'm going to let her find out that it's not true? Tonight's bit of acting there was a masterpiece. Don't forget your mother either,' he added with a look of annoyance. 'You seem to be not as bad as I thought at first—nevertheless, she needs to be removed from here, and you're going to help in that even if it is my money that will help her when in reality it should have been done ages ago with your money.'

Merissa never answered. In this kind of game she was useless. To say anything at all would bring her to the brink of a complete confession and then she would be really in his power. She looked down and said nothing.

'I'll collect both of you tomorrow at about ten,' he said firmly, still holding her in the loose but strong circle of his arms. 'We'll have lunch at the cottage and I'll sell your mother the idea. Don't mention it to her before then,' he warned sharply.

'I've told enough lies for one day,' she muttered, moving uneasily, trying to get free without a struggle and finding it not very easy.

'It comes to my mind that you've told no lies at all, except perhaps by omission,' he said quietly. 'If you think it over you'll realise that I did all the talking. You simply nestled in my arms like a sweet and dazed little angel, fathoms deep in love.'

'I *was* dazed!' she said hotly, her colour flaring as she remembered looking for so long into those blue eyes. 'I was dazed by your ability to lie at the drop of a hat!'

'And by my astonishing ability to kiss you into silence?' Julian asked wryly. 'I think that surprised both of us. Now I know what to do when you need a little disciplining. Every employer has to have some sort of control over the people he employs. I'm just lucky. Making you toe the line will be a pleasure.'

'You wouldn't dare!' she began, realising her mistake as he pulled her swiftly forward and captured her mouth in one smooth movement.

Now that they were standing without the awkward confines of the car to keep them apart, it was so much worse. He was ruthless, she thought breathlessly. He pulled her tightly against him with a speed that was frightening, almost as if he had been waiting for this moment since the shock of kissing her in the car. Certainly he was enjoying kissing her now, and after a second her ability to think receded into the distance. All she could do was feel, and he was making quite sure she did that, his hands moulding her to him with a pleasurable sensuality that was little short of shocking.

Merissa pulled her lips free, but she was given no time to

do more than gasp for air before she was captured again, his mouth plundering, his hand holding her head to his face, her hips to the surging hardness of his thighs.

'You—you're—disgusting!' she gasped as he at last released her, holding her loosely to allow her to come to her senses. She supposed she should be grateful for that, though, because if he had simply let her go she would have fallen. Nobody had ever held her like that before or kissed her like that—it was embarrassing, almost indecent.

'Disgusting?' Julian looked at her flushed face with vivid eyes. 'You want me to coax you? You look so surprised, Merissa. What a clever little actress you are! If I hadn't seen you with Goddard, I might even be apologising right now. Don't forget, though, I know his reputation with women, and even if I didn't I saw the look he gave you after that promotion. Was he remembering or anticipating?'

He seemed to be really angry now, and the arms that had for a few seconds been almost protective were like an uncomfortable prison from which she struggled belatedly.

'Is that why you said you wanted to take me away from him,' she managed scathingly, 'so that you could take his place?'

He scowled down at her in the dim lighting and she was almost sure she could see colour surge across his high cheekbones too.

'Take his place?' he growled angrily. 'Don't flatter yourself! I'm merely showing you the inadvisability of flexing your muscles with me. You can play nicely at being demure—keep it like that. Now we both know you have less nerve than I thought you had, maybe you get through by stealth and trickery. Don't try either of those tactics with me. I don't fool easily, and I know what I want. You'll be happy to know it damned well isn't you!'

Having got the last word as usual, Julian left, and Merissa went back into the house, pleading tiredness to avoid discussing him with her mother. She couldn't face questions—in fact, she couldn't even face herself. She was ashamed at the reactions he had forced from her when he held her, and she was frighteningly vulnerable, not at all sure how she was going to cope with things.

With the dawning of the new day, Merissa found that her mother was bright and cheerful. She had gone to a lot of trouble to get ready and she looked years younger.

'You look really pretty,' Merissa said with genuine pleasure as they both waited for fate in the form of Julian Forrest to arrive. 'I feel dull and dowdy at the side of you.'

Her mother's pleasure was all too clear, and for the first time since her father's death, Merissa allowed herself a little burst of hope. She remembered how her mother used to look when her father had been at the university. She had felt proud of her then as she did today, and she was glad of her own decision to dress more soberly. It was a chance for her mother to shine.

'Beautiful!' Julian remarked as he saw her mother, and it set the tone for the day. He had brought a bigger car today so that Mrs Troy would be comfortable, and she sat in the back as they left the city behind, chatting away to Julian about everything that came into her mind as Merissa sat in silence beside him.

'Not much traffic about,' he observed in a gap in the conversation. 'At this rate we'll be there in just over the half-hour. You're quiet this morning, darling,' he added, looking across at Merissa, his eyes on her dark trousers and sweater, her only concession to colour a bright scarf around her neck.

He meant that she looked reasonably dressed, she knew, and her quick glare had his lips twitching in amusement.

'She's tired,' her mother observed. 'She went straight to bed last night and never even wanted to talk about the engagement.'

'Well, she was only following orders,' Julian said comfortably. 'She reacts badly to excitement. It was too much for her.'

The sarcasm that her mother never heard infuriated Merissa, especially as she could do nothing to defend herself

with her mother sitting there so innocently. Her face
flushed uncomfortably when Mrs Troy continued, 'I hope
you realise what a wonderful and kind girl you have there!'

Julian's face was a picture of shock and stifled laughter as
he glanced across at Merissa.

'Oh yes,' he breathed softly, 'I know exactly what I've got
here.'

The cottage turned out to be a small but expensive country
house, the garden alive with colour and a smiling little
housekeeper waiting who had clearly been warned of their
arrival.

'Do you live here, Julian?' asked Mrs Troy as they went
over the house, her pleasure with it evident.

This is it, thought Merissa, almost holding her breath.

'No, not now,' Julian said quietly, motioning them to
chairs in the sunlit room at the front of the house. 'I'm
hoping, though, that you will live here in future.'

Mrs Troy just looked at him silently, her face a picture of
surprise, and he gave her no time to refuse, no time really to
react, the master planner as usual.

'Rose Cottage is my engagement present to Merissa,' he
said evenly with so much conviction that Merissa found
herself almost believing it. 'That's why I didn't want her to
do too much talking last night. We would both like you to
move in here and live here permanently—wouldn't we,
darling?' he added, looking across at Merissa.

'Yes, Mummy,' she managed, swallowing her own shock
and looking anxiously at her mother. He had put it in a way
that her mother could not refuse and she realised why he
was so good at his job. he had built this lie as he built his
constructions, piece by piece, every little part of it a part of
the whole grand finale, only in this case, a part of the whole
grand lie. She dared not look at him, her eyes were on her
mother's face, and she saw the pleasure and desire to live
here warring with the idea of possible charity.

'I really couldn't live in your house, Julian,' she said at

last, reluctantly, and he leaned forward and took both her hands in his.

'But you really can't refuse to live in Merissa's house, can you?' he asked with a smile. 'And this is Merissa's house now. My own house is at the other side of the city. We both want you to be here in the country air and we want you to get well and strong. It's not going to be very nice for you when Merissa moves out of that house and you're alone, and I'm determined she isn't going back there after this weekend.'

Don't tell her where I'm going, Merissa prayed. Let her recover from this shock before we get to the really shocking part of this. He didn't, and her mother didn't ask, instead her face flooded with pleasure.

'If you put it like that, then how can I refuse?'

'Good!' said Julian, giving her a hug. He was really getting into this part of the future son-in-law, Merissa thought sourly. She could almost hear the wedding bells. By the time this was over her mother would be convinced that the ending of this engagement was all her fault.

She voiced this dark thought rather waspishly to Julian as they walked together in the garden after lunch, her mother staying behind to talk to Mrs Boddy, with whom she seemed to have an instant affinity.

'We'll manage that as easily as we've managed everything else,' he assured her smoothly. 'So far, I'm very pleased. Things are going according to plan.'

'I'm sick of your damned plans!' Merissa snapped. 'You expect me to swallow the most appalling lies and back you up on the spur of the moment. You could have told me about my really wonderful engagement present last night!'

'I only got the idea last night,' he confessed, stopping and swinging her towards him. 'In any case, I was too busy when we were saying goodnight, wasn't I?' She stared at him angrily, willing her face to remain merely annoyed, and he added, 'Don't you realise that even at this distance it's perfectly possible to tell when someone is quarrelling? Having just talked your mother into living in more healthy and suitable surroundings, I can see very little sense in letting her see a battle between us and making her feel uncomfortable.

'She's not even looking in this direction!' she snapped, hastily looking round and then looking back at him with annoyance.

'She was, and will again,' he assured her. 'It's only natural, surely. Just learn to curb your little temper until she's well out of the way.'

'Very well,' she said with a certain amount of glee. 'That appears to give me *carte blanche* at all other times. I'll wait, then. I'll keep quiet now and save it all for later!'

'You'll certainly keep quiet,' he remarked acidly, pulling her against him. 'And failing the necessary privacy to put my hand over your mouth, this will have to do for now.'

I could get used to this, Merissa thought frantically as his lips closed over hers. It could become a habit. This time she dared not even struggle, because she was not at all sure where her mother was or when she would turn this way.

'Put your arms round my neck,' he said thickly against her ear. 'If she's watching she'll believe this for sure.' He pulled her more tightly against him, and Merissa gasped at her own body's reaction. It was becoming increasingly difficult to resist this, and though she knew she was outraged, her body felt a kind of sweet delight every time he touched her. She fought silently against this attraction. Here was a really ruthless man, her enemy, a man who had trapped her and who thought that the truth was not a thing to be given anything but a very slight consideration. She was going crazy!

She fought free and moved away, gasping, her eyes wide and angry.

'I won't perform for my mother's benefit!' she pronounced bitterly. 'You're the most . . .'

'I certainly am at this moment,' Julian interrupted ruefully, running his hand through his hair in an odd distracted manner. 'Let's join the grown-ups, shall we? I think I need moral support.'

Merissa closed her mouth tightly and turned away, beginning to walk off and only stopping with reluctance when he said her name softly.

'Merissa, I almost forgot—in the excitement.'

She swung back, ready to defend herself against any new attack, her cheeks pink, but he was not even looking at her. He had a box in his hand and he opened it as she stood a few feet away.

'Come here,' he ordered softly. 'I have to give you the ring. Your mother is expecting to see it today.' He looked up, meeting her eyes. 'It's quite safe to approach,' he added quietly. 'I think we've shown the flag enough in case she was watching. She's not going to expect us to be in a permanent clinch, she's sure to be the old-fashioned kind, and I suppose she fondly imagines you are too. Come on.'

She walked slowly forward, still wary. Almost everything he said was an insult, if not outright then certainly the innuendo was there. It took all her resolve not to flinch as he took her hand and slid the ring on to her finger.

'There's no need to recoil so very obviously,' he said with an angry look at her. 'I'm not going to make a habit of kissing you. Before long we'll be where no one will see us, then it won't be necessary to pretend!'

Merissa never answered. She was gazing at the ring in awe. It was nothing like the ring she had expected him to produce. She had thought it would be some great showy diamond as big as a bird's egg so that she could flash it under the noses of his unwanted girlfriends, but this ring was beautiful, a square-cut ruby surrounded by the glitter of small diamonds, the whole in an elaborate setting.

'It—it's beautiful,' she managed in a breathless voice. 'It looks old.'

'It is,' Julian assured her quietly. 'In fact, it's been in my family for years. It was my grandmother's. I'm very relieved it fits. There must be something of Cinderella in you—maybe I should have a glass slipper for you to try.'

'I don't think I feel very happy about wearing an old family ring,' she managed to get out in a choked little voice.

The implications of his remark made her heart thump uncomfortably, and he looked up with a sudden annoyance.

'I'm sorry if you preferred to have a brand new and flashy ring,' he rasped. 'Unfortunately, I didn't have any time to shop for one. We must make do with this.'

'I didn't mean that at all!' she flashed back at him, annoyed now herself that he managed to take everything the wrong way and come out with the worst whatever she said. 'I was only thinking it seemed to be wrong to wear this ring when the whole thing is a lie. One day you'll get engaged for real, and then this ring will be—be sort of . . . tarnished.'

'Tarnished?' Julian was giving her that odd look again and she met his gaze with clear eyes, her head held proudly.

'Yes, tarnished. I can't think of any other word that fits the bill. I'm wearing what's obviously an important ring, regardless of its value. When the time comes to give it to the person you really intend to marry, you'll remember this— this time and—and me. It will spoil it for you.'

He looked at her for so long that she had to look away, turning to face the house again so that he wouldn't see her flushed cheeks and the sudden flare of hurt in her eyes. She began to walk away, and he was immediately beside her, matching her pace, and his arm came warmly around her waist.

'You don't mind wearing it?' he asked quietly.

'No. I was only thinking of you, as it happens,' she muttered, keeping her face averted. 'It's a beautiful ring. Anyway,' she suddenly added, looking at him in a panic as a thought struck her, 'what if I should lose it? It does happen, you know, and in my job I'm taking things off and . . .'

Her voice died away at the amusement on his face and his arm left her waist as he took her hand firmly.

'Not while you wear my ring,' he reminded her quietly. 'You've got a new lifestyle now. Remember? You won't be required to—er—take things off.' She couldn't seem to think of any suitable retort and he led her to the house, obviously intent on the next step in his game.

Her mother loved the ring, creating a great fuss over it and insisting that Mrs Boddy looked too. It made Merissa feel guilty and disloyal to see so much happiness that was based solely on a lie, but her worries took a sharp new turn as Julian dropped his final bombshell when Mrs Boddy had hurried off to the kitchen.

'I'm really glad to see that you and Mrs Boddy have managed to be on such friendly terms so quickly,' he told Mrs Troy. 'You realise, of course, that she'll be staying on here to keep house for you—and of course I'll take care of her wages. She'll be company for you too. We don't want you to be alone at night.'

'Well, of course, I like her and I certainly wouldn't want her to lose either her job or her home,' said Mrs Troy. 'But naturally I'll have Merissa here at night too.'

'No. It's too far for Merissa to travel,' said Julian in a firm but matter-of-fact voice. 'She's going to be really busy with her new job and after the posters go up she'll be getting new and important contracts. She'll be living in my house. It's closer to the city.'

Shock and disapproval were written across Mrs Troy's face, but Julian ignored it and went on, 'Naturally, she'll have a chaperon. I also have a housekeeper.'

'Well...' Only partially mollified, Mrs Troy studied her hands for a moment and then looked up. 'I suppose young people nowadays ...'

'I imagine you can trust Merissa,' he said quietly and sincerely, 'and I'm thirty-six, old enough to have a little common sense.'

'Well—you're old enough to look after her,' she agreed slowly. 'Mind you, if it had been one of those scatterbrained young men she used to know when she was at university ...'

Once again Julian had pulled it off, and Merissa was dazzled by his ability to charm her mother and lie his way out of trouble. Now that it had been mentioned openly too, she was more anxious than ever at the prospect of staying in his house. It would be all right, so long as he didn't touch her . . .

He tackled her on the new knowledge he had acquired as they said goodnight when they were back at her house, her mother safely inside.

'You were at university?' he enquired with obvious surprise.

'Yes. I left in my second year.'

'Why?' He sounded suspicious, as if she had been thrown out for some horrid action. No doubt he was thinking that.

'My father died,' she snapped, her eyes suddenly bright with tears. 'Our source of income dried up.'

For a moment he was silent, and she took the opportunity to get in a request that she had been fearful to put to him earlier.

'When—when I'm working for you . . . Well—I mean . . .'

'Out with it, Merissa,' he ordered, reasonably enough. 'We may as well clear the air.'

'I'd like to continue modelling all the time,' she got in quickly, hurrying on when she saw danger in his eyes. 'I mean, when it's all over, I'll need a job, and if I leave it too long I'll be out in the cold. You can't stop when you're modelling. It's a short enough life as it is in the modelling world.'

'Very well,' Julian agreed after a moment's thought. 'But only the best jobs. Derrick Lean is very interested, and I suppose Clare Anders will push you now that he's shown an interest. The sight of the posters should inspire a good many people to call you too. Nothing cheap, though! I'll want to know what you're doing and why!'

'Thank—thank you,' Merissa whispered breathlessly, almost unable to believe this concession. She needed much more than fifteen thousand to pay off her father's debts, and her mother would never rest until it was done.

'I'll also buy your clothes,' he added in a sort of threatening voice. 'I want you to look expensive at all times, even when you go to a job.'

She was prepared to make any concession, having little choice anyway, so she simply nodded and looked down.

'Remember too,' he added in a harsh voice, 'that you're engaged!'

'I can hardly forget it,' she muttered, her eyes on the toes of her shoes, not at all surprised when he turned angrily away to his car.

'I'll be in touch with you,' he said shortly, and then he was gone.

To Merissa's surprise, Julian let things ride for over a week, leaving them both in the house where they had lived since soon after her father's death, not calling or phoning, disappearing as if he had never existed, until only the cold fact of the ring on her finger proved that he was real.

Hugh Goddard phoned, though, and though she had promised to keep well away from any male friends she found herself resentful and foolishly lonely. She also found herself agreeing to go to dinner with Hugh, telling herself it would of course be the last time.

It wasn't until they were sitting in the dim lighting of a small restaurant that Hugh pounced. She had been surprised at his choice of an eating place, his tastes normally running to the extravagant, but she soon realised he had wanted a quiet place so that he could be as furious as he pleased with few interested spectators.

'What's all this about you being engaged?' he demanded even before their meal was served, the words bursting from him with furious speed.

Merissa's eyes flew to her hand; for a moment she was afraid she had forgotten to remove the ring. She had not had any intention of telling Hugh, having battled it out with her conscience. He was, after all, merely a family friend, in spite of the rather daring things he sometimes said to her, and she could see no reason to spread the good tidings any further than necessary. Anyway, his attitude when he had seen Julian on both occasions had been peculiar, to say the very least, and she had as much trouble as she could cope with at the moment.

'Oh, I expect you've removed the evidence to come out with me,' he said angrily, his eyes following her anxious glance at her own hand. 'I'm surprised you can be so deceitful, Merissa. God knows what your father would have made of it!' Before she could reply he added with greater fury, 'Anyhow, you didn't need to bother. Forrest isn't keeping it a secret. It's in *The Times*—or don't you read *The Times*?' He glared across at her as she shook her head and added with disgust, 'Well, my dear, you're engaged to Mr Julian Forrest, according to *The Times*, and I can see by your guilty looks that it's true!'

'I'm not at all guilty!' Merissa said coldly, stung by his tone and the fact that he felt capable of speaking to her like this. 'I removed the ring because it's a family heirloom and I was afraid of losing it. I didn't feel it necessary to ask your permission to get engaged.'

'You damned well know how I feel about you!' he snapped, appearing to lose any control, his face white and drawn. 'Do you imagine you can fit in to the sort of world that Forrest occupies, you little fool? He's got a reputation that would frighten off any decent girl. If your father was alive ...'

'It's funny,' Merissa said angrily, her father's name filling her with grief and fury when taken so lightly. 'You've just said more or less exactly what Julian said about you! Maybe I should try to get to the bottom of this while I still can.'

'What did he say about me?' Hugh was suddenly not at all her old friend. His hand was painful as it fastened hers to the table and gripped cruelly. She pulled her hand away, watching him battle with a wild rage, her eyes taking in things she had never noticed before. There was a ruthless, almost vicious look on his face, and her realisation of it showed in her eyes.

'You hardly know the man,' he muttered, fighting for

control, clearly knowing he had gone too far. 'You've only just met him.'

'How on earth can you know about that?' she asked scathingly, her own anger well on top now. 'As a matter of fact, I've just been working for him, and it's not the first time I've seen him.

'Well, it's too soon to get engaged,' he growled angrily. 'You don't know him.'

'I don't know you either, Hugh,' she said quietly. 'I've just realised that you can know a person for years and still not really know a thing about them. I'd like to leave, I think.'

'You'll stay here and eat,' he snapped sourly. 'I've not finished with you yet.'

'Well, I've finished with you,' she said firmly, rising as the waiter came with their food. 'You can ring me when your temper is improved. Call me a taxi, please,' she added to the surprised waiter, leaving with him and giving Hugh no time to react.

She was shaking with annoyance and with shock. Until recently, she had been simply struggling with her life, and now after a very little time, she found herself knee-deep in mystery and a sinister web of deceit. Hugh was not just furious about the engagement, she realised that all too well. If he had felt any great attraction to her he had had plenty of opportunity to let her know. It had only been with the arrival of Julian on the scene that he had changed his tune, and he had lied about knowing who Julian was—that much was clear too.

As to Julian Forrest, he had taken the very first available chance to advise one and all that she was engaged to him— another of his little plans, she thought furiously. It took her all her time to get control of her rage before she got home, and even then she had to tell a lie, make an excuse of a headache to her mother who had not had the faintest idea where she had been anyway, for the first time in her life! She was enmeshed in the web like a small and stupid creature. It all made her feel rather tawdry and dirty.

Julian phoned at the end of the next day.

'Right! The posters are up,' he stated without preamble. 'Now you go into action! The engagement party is on Friday. Cancel any assignments you have for that day—I don't want you looking tired. On Wednesday I move your mother into Rose Cottage and you move in with me.'

'But . . .' Merissa only got out the one word.

'Nothing to worry about,' he assured her briskly. 'I'll see to the moving. You move into Creswell House on Wednesday morning and once I've got you settled I'll go back and get to your mother. I've already ordered the removal van—get your things packed separately. We'll shop for a dress for you on Friday.'

'Now look here——' she started, but he let her get no further.

'What's bothering you, Merissa?' he grated sourly. 'We've been through this before and I'm merely giving you the details. I don't need to really do all that as you're merely working for me. I feel very generous about the fact that I'm allowing you to take extra assignments, so don't push your luck!'

'You never said anything about an announcement in *The Times*!' she said bitterly. 'I imagined it would be kept in a small circle of people. You had no business to do that without consulting me!'

'How did you know?' asked Julian with sudden quiet. 'I didn't know you took *The Times*.'

'We don't! Somebody told me.'

'Who?' he pounced immediately, but she now hedged rapidly.

'Just somebody,' she snapped, trying to keep up her temper when the ground was beginning to feel decidedly uneven beneath her feet. 'It doesn't matter who it was, the thing that matters is—why did you do it?'

'Listen, you little shrew,' said Julian darkly. 'I do as I wish. All you have to do is obey orders and collect your pay. Follow my instructions to the letter. Goodbye!'

'I'm not a shrew!' she shouted, the fact that she was trying to keep her voice lowered adding to her annoyance. She didn't want to have to explain this lovers' quarrel to her mother.

'Then don't sound like one!' he bit out. 'It's lucky for you that I'm so far away, or I'd soon put an end to this childish rebellion!'

'Oh? I'd like to see you try!' she flashed back, then went red-faced as he burst into laughter.

'I'm beginning to think you would,' he said softly. 'The way you react to me is very gratifying. However, we'll go into that at some later date. Behave yourself, Merissa.'

He simply put the phone down, and Merissa clenched her fists in a fury. Damn the man, she couldn't seem to think about anything or anyone but him nowadays! It was something she would have to watch if she was to survive this ridiculous affair with her heart and mind still her own.

CHAPTER FIVE

CRESWELL HOUSE was a bit of a surprise. The fact that Julian had called a quite large country house a cottage had led Merissa to believe that something that he was prepared to call a house would in all probability be an Elizabethan mansion, but it was nothing like that.

It was modern, stone-built and very attractive, certainly a house of this century and clearly a creation by Julian Forrest. It stood in its own grounds in a quiet village well out of London and the stone walls that surrounded it had tall bushes growing inside the grounds, rising well above the walls, making for additional privacy. It was not a spectacular house, but it was big, modern and well designed, tasteful. Merissa had the feeling that he worked a lot from here, and found out that this was true after he had left her and gone off to help her mother to move to Rose Cottage.

The housekeeper was not after all any problem; she was as pleasant and unassuming as Mrs Boddy and, true to the air of rather remote self-reliance about Julian, Mrs Patterson was not the sort of woman who concerned herself with anything but her job. She shook hands with Merissa and then left to make coffee, allowing Julian to show Merissa to her room and settle her in, clearly being used to his ways. He was not the sort of man who would appreciate a fussy housekeeper who treated him as if she was a nanny.

'Well, what do you think of it?' he asked Merissa quietly as he deposited her suitcases in the room that was to be hers for the duration of her stay. It was at the back of the house, facing open country. It was luxurious, and after her normal, cramped bedroom she couldn't stop looking at it and walking round, a childish feeling of delight inside her that she tried to squash, reminding herself that this was nothing permanent and that it would be better to look upon the whole thing as a hotel.

'Remember me?' Julian's amused voice had her glancing quickly at him as he stood in the doorway. Her face flushed. In her excitement she had forgotten that he was still there looking at her, and she felt very stupid as well as childish.

'Cats do that,' he added as she did not answer. 'They go around in circles getting the feel of the place. Maybe I should butter your paws,' he added with a grin.' I really wouldn't like it if you decided to wander off to another home.'

It made her laugh and took away some of the embarrassment, and for once Julian seemed to be in accord with her, coming to look out of the window as she stood there.

'I can see you like it,' he said softly, 'and I'm glad to have both you and your mother housed in better circumstances. I'll leave you to get settled and then you can explore the house and surroundings. Keep out of mischief, though.'

His hand under her chin and his smiling eyes took the sting out of his words and she found herself smiling back, suddenly feeling completely at home.

'I'll take you out to dinner when I get back,' he promised, his hand still in possession of her chin. 'I'll tell Mrs Patterson, don't you bother about it.'

He looked down at her for a few minutes and she was sure he was about to kiss her. She wanted him to kiss her, she realised, and it must have shown on her face, because his own face was very warm and gentle.

'Perhaps after all, we'd better ration it,' he murmured. 'I'm beginning to think it's addictive!' Merissa knew what he meant, and he left her no time for embarrassment. He simply walked out of the room and left the house almost immediately afterwards.

She unpacked then went down to coffee in the lounge, exploring the whole place later and discovering a small sitting-room at the back of the house with French windows that opened on to the lawns. She knew it would be her favourite room at once, and looked up with a smile as Mrs Patterson walked in.

'This is a lovely room,' she said with soft appreciation.

'Yes, Miss Troy, I always think so myself. It's a ladies' room to the very inch. I sometimes wonder if it was a woman who planned the décor—it's a bit soft for Mr Forrest to have planned, I think.'

A lady? Who? Merissa suddenly found the idea not at all to her liking. Who had stayed in Julian's life long enough to have had a hand in this room? She was surprised at her own reaction. The thought hurt her! She had better remind herself more often that this was only a job and that she had been ruthlessly trapped into it. It would never do to begin to feel anything for Julian Forrest. He was out of her league—and anyway, she didn't like him at all.

He was still out at six o'clock when Mrs Patterson called her to the telephone and she heard her mother's voice at the other end.

'Julian asked me to let you know he's on his way back,' she said happily. 'Apparently you'll want to change for dinner as you're going out on the town. Honestly, Merissa, I thought he was never going to leave! He was so interested in your father's music tapes. He's going to come back soon and play them all!'

Merissa was surprised, for more than one reason. Her father had been an avid collector of tapes and to play them all would be quite a feat. Apart from that, her mother had never wanted them to be played after her father's death, so Julian must have coaxed her into letting him use them for some reason. This, too, puzzled her. She had had a look at Julian's extensive collection of records and tapes and they were almost all jazz, from some original old jazz records to modern masters of the sound. Her father had collected the classics.

She remained thoughtful all evening, and Julian too was very silent as he took her out to dinner.

Next day, though, there was a clash on a magnificent scale that drove away any thoughts of happiness in the comfort of Creswell House and showed the really frightening depths of Julian's temper.

They went to buy the dress for the engagement party, and he insisted on sitting there while Merissa modelled dress after dress in one of the most expensive shops, embarrassing her very deeply when he picked out six and paid for them all.

'About shoes and things——' he remarked with irritating interest as they walked down Bond Street later.

'I've got plenty,' she said with vexation, hoping the dresses would be delivered too late for the party but knowing, from the fawning expression on the face of the manageress and the size of the cheque that Julian had signed, that they would be there long before they got back; certainly they would be if he continued to do what he was doing now, lingering to look in shop windows.

She watched him for a minute before walking on ahead. He looked almost contented doing this, and she knew that at any moment he would dive into a shop and insist on buying her something else. She didn't want to be any further in his debt. When she left he would undoubtedly give her all the things he had bought for her, and she didn't want that. She knew that for some reason she would never want to see them again, not when they reminded her of Julian. It would be a very painful reminder, and she flatly refused to think about that at all. She was beginning to care about him, and she could not afford to do that.

She was so lost in thought, so utterly miserable about this new complication in her life, that she never saw Hugh. Only the fact that two hands came to her shoulders and she was swung round into two masculine arms brought her to earth with a sickening thud.

'Merissa!' He gave her a great hug before she could gather her wits and then draw back to stare into her face with a rueful expression on his. 'Merissa, love! I thought I'd never see you again. I've been ringing your house all morning and all day yesterday, and nobody answered. Where have you been? I didn't know what to do. Merissa, I'm so sorry about the other night—I never meant to yell at you like that. Surely you can understand how I felt, knowing that you were engaged? Will you forgive me?'

'I—well, of course I will.' Merissa was so stunned by his sudden appearance and by his complete change of mood that she stood there in his arms like a rag doll.

'I can't let you go, Merissa,' he said deeply, looking into her eyes with a pained expression on his face that astounded her. He had certainly changed. He was like another person, and every instinct rose up to protect her.

She didn't need such fragile protection. Reality in the form of two strong hands on her shoulders that drew her roughly back and away from Hugh shocked her into the fact that Julian had not been more than a few yards away and had certainly seen this little and astonishing meeting.

He drew her to his side, clamping her there with an arm like steel, his voice thick with fury.

'You'll let her go now or you'll find yourself incapable of standing!' Julian ground out angrily. 'If I ever see you near Merissa again, I'll take you apart!'

Anger and shock with the remembered touch of fear flooded Hugh's face, and suddenly Merissa was nothing more than a spectator in this silent battle. If before she had been suspicious then now she was sure that not only did they know each other but that the enmity ran very deep indeed and had little to do with her.

'I've known her all her life—well, for years, anyway,' snarled Hugh. 'Just because you've beaten me to it and got engaged to her it doesn't give you the right to . . .'

'To what?' asked Julian with a murderous quiet, his face white with rage. 'I have the right to protect her from undesirables, and you fit that category better than anyone I can think of. Stay away from her! If I so much as think even in my wildest moments that you're anywhere near her, I'll come after you with everything I've got!'

He spun Merissa round, taking her hand and marching her along leaving a furious and red-faced Hugh standing looking after them, and it was not for a few minutes that Merissa found her breath and her voice.

'You had no right . . .!' she began angrily, trying to keep her voice down as several passers-by were eyeing them with open speculation. They made a handsome couple and they were clearly angry with each other, even though Julian's tight grip on her hand had not relaxed.

'I have every right!' he bit out. 'I employ you, and to the rest of the world you're engaged to me! I said no men!'

'Even people who are really engaged keep in touch with their friends!' she answered stormily. 'This isn't the middle of the desert, you know. You can't kill anyone who looks at my face.'

'A damned good job!' he snapped. 'I couldn't think of a better fate for Goddard!' He pushed her into the car and drove off furiously, and she was too frightened and astonished to say anything else. It was like being in a maze, not knowing where she was or how she had got there. Something was very, very wrong, and she had not one clue as to what it was, but certainly she had inadvertently stepped into someone else's drama and she was playing a role without being told the lines.

He couldn't keep his violence bottled in, though. When

they were on a quiet stretch of road a few miles from Creswell House, he pulled into the side of the road and switched off the engine, turning to her angrily.

'OK!' he rasped. 'Just what is he to you?'

'I've told you, I think,' muttered Merissa, keeping her eyes on the fields at her side of the car, hiding her face effectively. 'He's an old friend, a friend of the family, as it happens. If you'd been listening when you came to tea with us you would have heard my mother say that he too came to tea, one of our very few visitors, almost the only one who's stuck by us since . . .'

She suddenly realised just what she was saying and stopped very swiftly, biting her lip in vexation. That was just about the last thing she was going to tell him.

'I asked what he is to you!' Julian ground out, grasping her chin and turning her face towards him so that he could see her eyes. 'You're little more than a girl and you've been going around with somebody like that! Don't tell me you don't know what he's like, because I won't believe it. Women who know him are not to my liking.'

'I'm engaged to you, and you're only saying what Hugh said about you the other night when I . . .' Merissa stopped as his face flared with anger, her fear rising as she saw her mistake.

'So!' he hissed, dragging her close to him. 'Since our trip to Rose Cottage you've been out with that—that . . .'

'I didn't wear the ring,' she said hastily, appeasement her only thought, and that really drove him over the top.

'I bet you didn't, you little bitch!' He glared down into her eyes, his own eyes brilliant pools of burning blue. 'I can see why you were afraid of losing it when you had to take things off. There's not much chance of keeping things on with Goddard, is there!'

Even at such close quarters Merissa managed to put a great deal of force into the sharp slap that she delivered across his cheek, not at all remorseful to see her finger marks etched in red across his face. Before he could react she was out of the car and storming off along the deserted road, going doggedly on even when she heard the car door slam and Julian's footsteps behind her.

'It's a good job you had the presence of mind to remove yourself for a few seconds,' he said quietly, taking her shoulders as he caught up with her and swinging her round, his temper now under control. She could see the marks on his face, but she quickly looked away, staring over his shoulder.

'I've just resigned!' she said firmly. 'You can take the slap as a written resignation. You may now do as you wish— even for my mother, I won't face that sort of thing. She wouldn't expect me to, and we'll be no worse off than we've ever been. I'll walk to the nearest telephone and call a taxi. You can send my things back to the house, we've not yet given notice to quit, so it's all right.

'Look, Merissa,' Julian began with a gentleness that had her puzzled for a moment—only for a moment, though. She had a sort of grip on him now, he had told that Louise person that they were engaged. He had told Hugh, an enemy, and he had told her mother. She couldn't help thinking he was fond of her mother for some reason or other; his attitude had been too genuine to be totally without feeling.

'It's very little use talking to me, Mr Forrest,' she said quietly. 'I have to put up with a great many things in my life and in my job, but nobody has yet accused me of being promiscuous, nobody but you, and I couldn't possibly work with you or for you.'

She couldn't move away, because he had a hard grip on her still, but she made it quite clear by her attitude that she had finished the discussion.

'I don't think that at all,' he said softly. 'I know experience when I see it, and you're like an innocent child when I touch you. I'm sorry I said all that—I was so damned mad, and I sometimes can't keep my temper. Whatever I may have thought when I first saw you, I know now that it wasn't true. Let's start again. I'm sorry.'

'I'm sorry too,' she said quietly, looking up at him, 'but I can't start again—there's a limit to how much I can stand. Goodbye, Mr Forrest.'

'Oh, Merissa,' he groaned softly, 'you don't leave me with much alternative, do you?'

Before she could work that out he had scooped her up into his arms and was striding back the few yards to his car, passing motorists blowing their horns and one even slowing down to give a long low whistle.

'Put me down!' snapped Merissa, her face red. 'I don't see that this is going to help. I'm not going to become happily settled because you choose to humiliate me further!'

'I'm not humiliating you,' he assured her as he let her stand beside the car. 'What I'm doing is capturing you. Now let's go home and talk like sensible adults. I'm not letting you dash off just because I lost my temper. I was as jealous as hell!'

'Jealous!' She stared at him as if he was mad, and he looked at her blandly, no sign of embarrassment on his face.

'Jealous!' he assured her with a nod of his head. 'Come on now, kitten. You knew I wanted you when I first saw you, you're not that innocent. I told you outright that I wanted to take you from Goddard. How do you suppose I felt when I saw you today locked in his nasty arms?'

'But—but—you said that—that ... This job ...' she stammered wildly.

'Ah, the job. Well, that's different,' he said firmly, opening the car door and bundling her inside while she was still too dazed to protest. 'The job is genuine enough.' He came round and got in beside her, turning to her at once, and she drew back immediately, a little wild-eyed.

'Don't you touch me!' She pressed herself against the door, and he burst into genuine laughter.

'Hell, I wasn't going to,' he laughed. 'Don't put ideas into my head. I'm not constantly on the prowl and I'm only just recovering from temper. I want to get you home and then we'll have a talk.'

'There's nothing to talk about,' she said, blushing

furiously. 'If you imagine for one moment that I'll agree to—to . . .'

'To what?' asked Julian, all wide-eyed innocence. 'You have a job to do for me, and I have something to tell you that's long overdue.'

'Tell me now!' she demanded, giving him a hard look and not allowing herself to think even for a moment about the—other thing.

'Very well.' He looked at her for a long moment and then sat back, reaching for a cigarette and taking a deep breath. 'I know who you are. I didn't at first. I saw you with Goddard and I was quite prepared to try and take you away from him. However, nothing is as easy as that, it seems. After the promotion at Fitzpatrick's when you literally ran out on me, I naturally asked your agent who you were. Troy isn't really a very common name. I got her to admit that you were in fact John Troy's daughter. I already knew that Goddard used to be his business manager, so it was easy to see that you'd simply kept up an association with him. Don't bother to deny that you're John Troy's daughter either.'

'I wasn't going to deny it!' cried Merissa, tears in her eyes. 'I'm not ashamed of Daddy, because none of the things they said about him in the papers is true. Mummy and I will never believe it. He was a wonderful man!'

'He was,' Julian agreed soberly. 'A very exceptional man at all times.'

'You knew my father?' She stared at him with tears on her face, and he looked away across the fields, nodding in agreement.

'I knew him,' he said with controlled savagery. 'I knew him very well.'

'How did you know him?' She felt on very uneven ground now, not knowing how to place Julian in her father's life. It made a difference now to her attitude to him, and she wished he hadn't said anything about wanting her. Maybe they could have played his whole scheme out now as friends. He had more or less made that impossible with his admission.

'It's a long story,' he said vaguely, his mind clearly elsewhere. 'I do know, though, that the things they said about him can't be true. Still,' he added, throwing the half-smoked cigarette away and starting the engine, 'that's another story. For now, though, keep clear of Goddard—and behave yourself.'

'I hope you'll do likewise,' Merissa said cuttingly, sniffing away the few remaining tears.

'All right,' he agreed. 'Dry your tears, then. Don't tempt me to kiss you better.' She dried them with a great deal of speed, and his laughter was quiet and annoying.

The dresses had arrived when they got back and Mrs Patterson had put them in Merissa's room, leaving her to unpack them and hang them herself. It was a very doubtful pleasure now. Hanging them up, she began to feel very uneasy, as if Julian was buying her, and although she told herself she would need them for the job he had in mind, still her puritanical mind advised her that he was staking a claim that she should resist with a stiff face and an outraged manner.

She was standing looking at them as they hung in the wardrobe when Julian strolled into the room, his eyes on her anxious face.

'Now what?' he asked in amusement. 'You've decided you want the whole lot exchanged for something different?'

'No! I'm not pleased to have any of them at all,' she snapped. 'I don't like you providing me with clothes!'

'It's for a job, not to buy your virtue,' he grinned, reading her expression easily and adding to her annoyance and discomfort. 'You're far too touchy, Miss Troy.'

'I won't need all these!' she snapped at him. 'I intend to be out of your life with all possible speed. I intend to slam into your friends and get out of here fast.'

'Ladies do not "slam into" people,' he informed her wryly. 'They insinuate coolly—and in any case, we both know you're not capable of slamming in to anybody, with the possible exception of me.'

'Look, just go and leave me in peace,' Merissa managed, turning away.

'Why do you always hide your face away?' he asked, coming closer. 'I always seem to be upsetting you. I'll soothe you like I did when your mother gave me that lovely tea-party.'

'No!' She began to move away, but his hands spun her round, his eyes holding hers with ease as he moulded her slim shoulders, and what little peace of mind she had oozed away as his thumbs probed the collar of her blouse. 'You— you're the last person to be soothing,' she got out, by sheer willpower. She had a ridiculous urge to press her lips to the hard, strong line of his neck that was so close now, and the weakness in her legs was steadily growing, moving upwards, making breathing difficult.

'Try me,' said Julian huskily, his fingers flexing on her shoulders like the restless paws of a tiger. 'Let's conduct a few experiments into human behaviour.'

He wasn't really thinking about his words. Even in her state of weak and trembling panic Merissa knew that. She couldn't seem to fight the waves of excitement that shook her either, and she wished something would happen to break the almost painful waves of feeling that were growing inside her.

Julian moved his hands from her shoulders and she had a sudden shock of disappointment that he was no longer touching her. Stop it! her mind warned her frantically, but it seemed to make little difference, and her breath left her in an audible sigh as Julian ran his finger with a tantalisingly light touch along her jawline.

'Please!' She gasped out the word as his hands came warm and possessive to cup her face and lift it to his. He said nothing, but his fingers tangled in her hair as he ignored the soft and yielding body so close to his. He seemed to be listening for signals, waiting, and she felt an urgent and mad need to be closer.

It only needed the little sound of torment from deep in

PLAY THE "LUCKY 7" SLOT MACHINE GAME!

NO COST! NO OBLIGATION TO BUY! NO PURCHASE NECESSARY!

PLAY "LUCKY 7"
AND GET AS MANY AS SIX FREE GIFTS...

HOW TO PLAY:

1. With a coin, carefully scratch off the silver box at the right. This makes you eligible to receive one or more free books, and possibly other gifts, depending on what is revealed beneath the scatch-off area.

2. You'll receive brand-new Presents® novels. When you return this card, we'll send you the books and gifts you qualify for absolutely free!

3. Unless you tell us otherwise, every month we'll send you 8 additional novels to read and enjoy. If you decide to keep them, you'll pay only $1.99 per book*, a savings of 26¢ per book. There is no extra charge for postage and handling. There are no hidden extras.

4. When you join Harlequin Reader Service, we'll send you additional free gifts from time to time, as well as our newsletter.

5. You must be completely satisfied. You may cancel at any time just by dropping us a line or returning a shipment of books at our cost.

* Terms and prices subject to change.

DETACH AND MAIL CARD TODAY

BUSINESS REPLY CARD

First Class   Permit No. 717   Buffalo, NY

Postage will be paid by addressee

Harlequin Reader Service®
901 Fuhrmann Blvd.,
P.O. Box 1867
Buffalo, NY 14240-9952

NO POSTAGE
NECESSARY
IF MAILED
IN THE
UNITED STATES

her throat and he had what he had been waiting for. He slid his arms around her and his mouth fused with hers hungrily with a demand that left her knees sagging, and she knew at that moment how very vulnerable she was as far as Julian was concerned. He could play with her emotions and then stand back and smile. He was used to this, to getting what he wanted, and it meant nothing at all except the satisfying of a desire that he had made no attempt to deny this afternoon.

She struggled belatedly and he lifted his head, the smile on his face that she had half expected.

'Changed your mind?' he asked softly, his eyes skimming her flushed face. 'Don't you know it's very dangerous to tease a man and then try to call it all off?'

'I didn't!' Merissa stared at him with wide dark eyes. 'It was you! It's always you, and you don't feel a thing!'

His answer was to pull her closer until her body was as fused with his as her lips had so recently been. There was no mistaking his arousal, and he was utterly unashamed of it.

'Don't I?' He ran one strong hand down her back, pressing her hips to his, and his eyes were no longer smiling. 'I can't really believe you're unaware of the affect you have on a man. You react instantly. Maybe it's your trick, this innocence. How many times did you sleep with Goddard?'

'I didn't!' She struggled wildly, but he held her fast, not teasing any more but hard and dangerous. 'You think you can say anything to me, don't you?' she cried bitterly. 'You think you can behave in any way you like because I'm trapped in this. You don't know why I ...'

'I'll know a whole lot more about you before long,' he murmured, his grip relaxing, 'and if I behaved as I liked I'd lock the door and put everything out of your mind but me.'

'That's what all this is about, isn't it?' she asked, feeling utterly lost when he moved away with an angry abruptness. 'There's really no job at all, it's just some nasty trick to get me here.'

'There's a job all right,' he snapped, looking at her with thoughtful eyes. 'One day I'll tell you exactly what it is, but not now, my little tease. You're much too prone to opening your beautiful mouth and saying the first thing that comes into your head. When you learn to think first and speak second, then you'll be a little more grown up.'

'Like Louise Atherton!' she blurted, then blushed furiously.

'Exactly!' he answered with a grin, his temper restored. 'I see you take my point. There's really no need to be jealous of Louise, though, you're here to get rid of her, remember?'

'I'm not jealous of anyone!' raged Merissa. 'And will you please leave? I have the right to privacy in this job, surely? I don't want to see you unless it's necessary.'

'Fortunately,' he laughed, 'it's going to be necessary to see a whole lot of me—employer's perks.' To her annoyance, he winked at her and walked out with a wide grin.

She sat down on the edge of the bed and considered her plight, her face still hot as she remembered her mindless enchantment when he touched her, her deep and growing need. He made her feel everything she had ever imagined it was possible to feel, and he was playing with her emotions with wry amusement. She couldn't afford to let her guard down for one minute. It would be madness to fall in love with him, but she wrapped her arms round her trembling body and rocked back and forth in an age-old instinct of self-comfort. What were the feelings she had now?

As she got ready for dinner she thought about almost anything to keep her mind off Julian, and naturally her thoughts went back to her father. She realised it was quite possible for Julian to have known her father well without her mother having the least idea about it. They were, after all, in almost the same line of business. Her father had been a specialist in concrete construction, world-renowned for his expertise in the chemical stabilisation of cement and the stress factors in building. All budding architects had wanted to get into his lectures, even coming from overseas to hear his ideas.

The collapse of Roman Point, the extensive problems on

motorway bridges and the collapse of a shopping mall bridge in America had, however, lured him away from an academic life into industry. He had talked about it for a long time before he had made the plunge and joined Ponton's. He had wanted to put his ideas into practice and see that things were being done. He was an idealist and he would not give ground either. Merissa supposed the same thing ran in her too, making her face life and carry on when things had become so very bad.

It melted her anguish to realise that Julian did not believe the things that had finally been said about her father, and she felt a deal of gratitude towards him. She knew he could be a good friend, a warm and loyal person to rely on. Not for her, though. He had chosen her for a job and he had ruthlessly trapped her into it without thought for her feelings, and this new aspect of things that he had so unashamedly admitted was frightening. It would be so very easy to sink into the emotions she felt for him, and she knew she would never survive then. She had to play him at his own game and get out of the situation finally with her heart and mind still intact. This was merely an episode, and her life had to go on as before when it was all over.

Still, she might as well try to find out things about her father that had puzzled her for so long. It had never been possible to question her mother, the hurt was still too close to the surface, and she had just let things drift from her mind in the day-to-day struggle to survive. Now, however, the heaviness of the burden had been partially lifted by Julian. For a while, she was comfortable, well paid, and her mother was taken care of. Everything was now in very sharp focus, and in any case, she would rather face the idea of trying to wheedle information from Julian than linger on the thought of his arms around her.

She got ready for dinner, struggling with her growing unhappiness, and went down to face him as if their brief interlude had never been. He was acting in exactly the same way, and Merissa took the opportunity to bring up the subject of her father as they dined for the first time at Creswell House.

'Julian——' she began carefully.

'Ah,' he said softly, looking across at her with amused eyes. 'You want something—that's the coaxing tone. I like it—carry on.'

'I was going to say,' she explained, ignoring his amusement, 'that I'd like to talk about my father.' Julian glanced at her in surprise and then continued eating.

'What do you want me to say to that?' he enquired a trifle stiffly, the amusement dying from his face. 'At one time I knew him very well indeed, too well to believe anything that's been said about him.'

'There are some things that I don't know,' she persisted. 'I need to know. Why, for example, did he leave Ponton's and set up in business by himself? It was a surprise enough when he left the university to go into the business world—but then to leave and set up on his own was surely a very big stride, and not in his line at all.'

'When he did that, I was out of the country,' said Julian with some reluctance, his eyes slightly puzzled on her face, 'but I know why. They were cutting corners.'

'What do you mean?'

'You're determined to get all this, aren't you?' he sighed, leaning back and looking straight at her. 'You'll probably not understand any of it.'

'I want to understand. Please, Julian!'

'How can I refuse when you look like that?' he said wryly. 'OK, I'll try to explain. Your father's field was the stress factor in building and he was rightly obsessive about safety. He went to Ponton's to see his ideas put into practice, to see them carried out to the very end. He thought, it seems, that if he actually showed his ideas working then they would be carried out worldwide and we wouldn't have these tragedies that happen from time to time. They cheated. He would give instructions for a fifty per cent overload factor to be built in, and when the designs and plans had been accepted, they were changing them. The site engineer would be told to build in only a twenty per cent overload factor. It saved millions. He found out.'

'How do you know?' persisted Merissa, forgetting to eat in her eagerness for this news.

'I have a contact,' he said quietly, 'and if you don't mind, I don't want to discuss this at the moment.'

He clearly meant it, and she didn't want to have any argument with him. At least she knew a little more now, and she couldn't see her father having left quietly either.

'He was working on a new thing, even when he was at the university,' she offered. 'Something about the water content. Something big.'

'I know.' Julian looked up quickly and stared at her hard. 'He never got it finished, though, did he?'

'I don't know. I suppose not,' she said, looking away from his suddenly keen gaze. 'We'll never know, anyway.'

Suddenly she didn't want to talk about it any more. The discussion had brought her father back vividly to her mind and she could see herself with him, visiting all the old historic buildings that had so fascinated him, listening to his voice. That was where she had got her desire to read history at university, and she supposed that had she been a boy she might well have followed in his footsteps.

'You'll have to let him go, Merissa.' Julian's voice brought her back to the present. 'It's been a long time now. The mourning should be over.'

'You don't understand!' she said sharply. 'It's not possible to forget when every day ...' There she was again, speaking first and thinking later. In that Julian was right. She would have to watch her tongue if she was not to disclose her terrible vulnerability. He never missed anything either. Right now he was watching her narrow-eyed, and she looked hastily down at her plate.

'There you go again,' he said quietly, 'hiding those expressive eyes. I want to get into your head, Merissa. I want to know all about you.'

'It—it won't be necessary,' she assured him hastily. 'There's nothing to know in the first place, and in the second place, remember that this is merely a job. The photographers don't want to read my mind.'

'They don't live with you,' he said innocently. 'I do.'

'Only because it's convenient!' she blurted out, looking away again as he grinned wickedly.

'I've not noticed a lot of convenience yet,' he said softly. 'I'll hope to collect my bonus later, perhaps. By the way,' he continued before she could take that up, 'my parents won't be able to attend the engagement party after all. As you know, your mother has very wisely begged off too. That being the case, we'll have to stand back to back against trouble. Think you can handle it?'

Merissa managed only a brief nod. Her mother had a good reason, the move had tired her and she was not too well just now but as far as she knew there was nothing to prevent Julian's parents from coming, except perhaps their disapproval. They were staunchly on the side of this girl Felicity, and she knew that facing them was going to be her biggest problem. Felicity wouldn't be at the party either; she was probably heartbroken. To be led on by Julian and then dropped abruptly and so cruelly would be enough to break any heart. She looked across at him and her own stomach twisted in sudden pain. She too was jealous— jealous that the strong, capable hands that had held her had also held Felicity, held her long enough and tenderly enough for her to imagine he would marry her.

Julian glanced up and caught the expression on her face, and goodness knew what he read there, but there was a bright and assessing light in his eyes and a half smile on his lips when she hastily went back to her meal.

'What did I do to deserve that look?' he asked quietly. 'I'm trying to analyse it at the moment and I'll certainly fathom it eventually. Want to save me some trouble and tell me now?'

'I wasn't thinking anything,' she lied swiftly. 'I was only mulling over about the party.'

'Yes,' he said in a voice that told her he was not at all deceived, 'I can see now that you were.' His quiet laughter ran like a finger of flame down her spine.

CHAPTER SIX

FRIDAY evening brought another clash with Julian, but to her great astonishment, Merissa won. He gave in and bowed to her judgement.

It was the matter of the dress. Julian wanted her to wear the white dress after all, disregarding the fact that they had spent a considerable time buying the six dresses that now adorned her wardrobe and that he had spent a considerable sum of money on them.

She had just showered and was standing doing her face, her white dressing gown securely belted, her still wet hair drawn back in a towel that hung down her back, when he knocked briefly and walked in.

'About tonight's clothes,' he announced arbitrarily as she opened her mouth to order him out. 'I want you to wear the white dress you modelled.'

'No!' She turned back to the mirror and kept silent, but she could imagine the look on his face.

'I must be hearing things,' he murmured softly, an edge to his voice. 'I thought for a moment there that you said no. I realise, though, that you couldn't have, because you're working for me, doing exactly as you're told for a very great deal of money. I'll begin again. I want you to look exactly as you looked when you were being photographed. I want you to be the same girl who's staring so beautifully out at everyone in London from those posters. The white dress!'

'No!' Merissa repeated, this time turning to look at him. She had herself well under control as far as he was concerned now, she thought thankfully. A sleepless night and she had sorted it out. It was only proximity. After he had gone from her life she would be able to forget him within days. It gave her confidence. 'In the first place, it would be so obvious that I'm astonished you could make a slip like that—you with all your cunning! They'll think I own the one dress, someone hired for the evening, Rent-a-Girl! No woman will miss an error like that. Naturally, though,' she added sweetly, turning back to the mirror and continuing with her make-up, 'if your decision is final, then I'll have to wear the dress—after all, I'm only here briefly, for the money. Don't blame me, though, if they ask where you hired me and come with their cheque books for a day or two of my time. It could pay better than photographic work.'

That went down like a lead balloon, and she heard Julian's angry hiss of breath in the deep silence.

'Very well,' he agreed after a moment, having clearly controlled that violent temper. 'I'll leave it to you as you're the expert—but as to your last remark,' he added with a very hostile note in his voice, 'don't let me catch you fluttering those long lashes at anyone or I'll put Plan B into effect!'

'What's Plan B?' she asked daringly, turning and fluttering her lashes at him in a moment of sheer impudence. It was suddenly exhilarating to tease him, to see his tight face when she had suggested that she might well pick up other work from the men there. It was suddenly exhilarating too to realise that Julian felt a desire for her that was only just beneath the surface, sufficiently close to the top to let his temper boil over at the mere suggestion of another man. It partly made up for the heartache he was beginning to give her.

'Plan B?' he murmured. 'That's the last alternative.' He looked at her for a long and silent minute until she turned away blushing, then he laughed softly. 'Ah,' he added with satisfaction, 'the coquetry is over, I see—back to the nun!'

He walked out, and Merissa added up her gains and losses and decided she was in fact steadily and quietly losing all the way along the line. She decided on the lemon dress, and as a concession did her hair exactly as she had it on the posters. Julian noticed.

'Clearly the expert,' he remarked as she came downstairs to find him waiting in the hall, handsome and sardonic as usual, his dinner jacket showing off the power of his shoulders. 'Lemon suits you—I noticed that before in Philip Swift's studio. There's not so much of the tan showing this evening, though. Come and fix my tie,' he added quietly.

'It's perfectly all right,' she said sharply, not wanting to stand that close.

'I don't think so. It feels a bit odd. See what you can do,' he said with an airy finality that left her with very little choice. She walked reluctantly over to him and put her evening bag down, turning to look at the tie. It wasn't quite straight after all. She unfastened it and began again.

Standing so close made her legs shake. Julian was a man to be kept at a distance, she thought as the faint tangy smell of aftershave drifted into her nostrils. He seemed to be towering over her, and she knew he was watching her with amusement.

'You have very strange and beautiful eyes,' he said softly. 'Neither your father nor your mother could have passed on eyes like that. I wonder where you got them!'

'Any large department store,' she said with shaky flippancy. The evening was worrying her enough without this, and in her haste to get away, she fumbled.

'If it's beyond you, I can do it myself,' he told her with quiet amusement, his hands coming lightly to her waist. 'Don't be so scared. You know I'll take care of you, don't you!'

'Maybe that's exactly what I'm scared of,' she said tartly and unwisely.

'What's to be scared about?' he asked softly, his hands tightening on her waist. 'If you had an affair with me, you would only gain by it, and there's one thing for sure, I wouldn't have to hire someone to get rid of you. You're definitely not the hard and clinging variety, although I could do with a little clinging at the moment.'

'Why are you saying things like this?' demanded Merissa

hot-faced. 'You said that once we were here we wouldn't have to pretend. There'll be no need to be—be . . .'

'Locked in a fond embrace?' Julian asked helpfully. 'Well, you know how I can lie! I only wanted to get you here. Now that you're here I don't seem to be getting what I'd bargained for. You're much too demure and shy for my liking. How am I ever to get you into my bed at this rate?'

She looked up at him in horror and found to her great annoyance that he was actually laughing, quietly and with great enjoyment.

'You're a really hateful man!' she snapped, stepping back and turning away to get her bag, and he never even replied, he simply took her arm and led her to the door, calling a cheery goodnight to the housekeeper and leading Merissa out to the car. He never mentioned the incident again and after a few seconds was talking as if it had never happened. If this was the sort of thing he did often then no wonder he needed help to sort out his love life! Merissa thought grimly.

The sight of the well known hotel frightened her enough, without the knowledge that all eyes were going to be on her as everyone Julian had invited tried to get a good view of the girl he had eventually decided to marry.

There was a private room reserved for them, and as the guests came in and shook hands with them both, she wished her mother had been there with her. She needed moral support. It was difficult enough without the very possessive attitude Julian had adopted. She realised he had to play the part, but as his arm stayed around her and his lips drifted across her cheek at every available opportunity, she couldn't help but think he was overplaying his hand. That he had ulterior motives with regard to herself, she would not even think about at all.

And of course, there was Louise Atherton! She never left them for a moment after arriving, and Merissa was beginning to think they had her with them for the rest of the evening.

'I've been trying to place you since I first saw you,' she said sweetly to Merissa as they moved at last away from the door. 'You're the girl on those great big posters one sees everywhere.' She turned and smiled up at Julian. 'Now don't tell me, darling, you're going to marry a model!' Her little smile told him she knew it was all some sort of joke.

'As soon as possible,' he said emphatically. 'Having fought my way to the head of the queue, I'm getting her securely bound before she escapes me.'

'Well, certainly your money will help her in her job,' said Louise with sweet malice. 'It's odd that I've never seen her before, and now that you're engaged her face is about the most noticeable thing in London.'

'She's not going to need a job, though, Louise,' Julian said pleasantly. 'I'll be quite enough for her to handle, won't I, sweetheart?' he added, looking down at Merissa's tight face.

'It looks as if you're more than she can handle right now,' Louise commented acidly. 'She's like a small ghost, not quite the radiant fiancée, darling.'

'Ah, we had a bad night,' Julian confessed, taking Merissa's hand and raising it to his lips. 'I think the bed's too small. I'll have to do something about it.'

Merissa's blushes were more convincing than any words she could have said, and Louise went white to the lips.

'She's at Creswell House?' she asked, glowering at Merissa.

'Where else would she be, for God's sake?' asked Julian irritably, swinging Merissa away as someone called to him, leaving Louise staring angrily after them.

'Why did you say that?' asked Merissa in trembling annoyance.

'To add reality to the thing for the benefit of someone who's not at all convinced,' he said shortly. 'Anyway, what's wrong with a bit of wishful thinking? I'm allowed the odd dream, surely?'

'It's certainly an odd one,' she snapped. 'You need psychiatric help!'

'That's not the sort of help I need at all,' he whispered, tilting her face and kissing her heartily, to her utmost embarrassment.

She found, though, that things were not as bad as she had feared. With Louise temporarily silenced, the others accepted her readily, and she found to her surprise that Julian knew some very nice people. They were mostly married couples, and she managed very well, gingerly letting her guard down as the evening progressed and simply being herself. Julian was pleased, she could see, and his eyes were never far away from her, until she almost felt that this was real.

The nightmare began later in the evening, though. She felt the itching start soon after she had eaten and she was dancing with an old friend of Julian's, Julian having been collared by Louise for a dance which he was clearly not enjoying and from which he escaped very quickly to go back to the bar with a group of others. Merissa knew immediately what the itching was—her allergy! It was the only one she had, but when it hit her she knew about it in a big way.

She felt in her bag as soon as she was able to get to the powder-room, and her heart sank. The anti-histamines she always carried were not there. Changing house, the upset of being with Julian, everything had conspired to make her forget habits long established. She had no defence against the growing allergic reaction.

She went to find Julian, knowing she would have to get out of here fast, and came up behind him, touching his sleeve.

'Julian.' He spun round quickly at the urgency in her voice, the mocking smile that he seemed to reserve exclusively for her dying on his face as he saw her flushed cheeks and shaking hands.

'What is it?' There was concern immediately but tinged with a slight annoyance. 'Don't tell me you've been drinking yourself senseless the moment you were out of my sight!'

'Julian, please!' whispered Merissa, her teeth chattering in spite of her attempt to stop—the next stage in an attack like this. 'I-I've g-ot to g-et out of here! I'm having an—an allergic ...'

She didn't need to say more. He looked hard at her and his hands came down on her shoulders, feeling the shaking.

'Can you manage to get to the car while I explain?' he asked urgently, giving her his keys as she nodded. 'I'll be a minute,' he said, turning her to the door. That was just about all he was, but by the time he came she was shivering and burning, her skin on fire.

'What is it!' Julian asked worriedly as he slid into the car and started at once after a worried glance at her.

'Almonds.' If she held herself absolutely taut she could control the chattering of her teeth at this stage, but soon she knew her whole body would be shaking uncontrollably.

'There were no almonds,' he assured her, but she shook her head, not wanting to talk.

'Even a little flavour would do it.' He could see she had clenched her teeth and was trying to get the reaction under control, and he went at a speed that required all his skill.

'Don't talk, Merissa,' he advised. 'My doctor will be there when we get back to the house. One of my friends has rung him for me, the same person who's explaining our sudden departure.'

'I—I'm sorry!' He stopped her at once, his hand coming to cover both of hers as they lay clenched in her lap.

'Stop worrying. Just hang on,' he said quickly. 'We'll be there soon.'

Not soon enough. By the time they pulled up in front of the house behind the doctor's car, Merissa was burning in every place possible, her skin irritating to such an extent that she was scratching all the time.

'Allergic reaction,' the doctor said briefly as soon as he saw her. 'What?'

'Almonds,' Julian replied before she could speak. 'God— look at her!' Merissa was in no condition to worry about how she looked, and in any case, she knew. Her skin was bright red all over and she was shaking like someone in a high fever.

'How much has she been drinking?' the doctor asked, diving into his bag. 'I'll have to inject her with antihistamine.'

'A glass of white wine at dinner, about two hours ago,' said Julian promptly, obviously having monitored her consumption. 'What later?' he asked, looking down at her.

'N-nothing. I—I don't d-drink.'

'Hold her completely still,' ordered the doctor, looking up at the light, preparing the injection, and Julian pulled her tightly into his arms, holding her bare arm rock-steady.

'Another virtue?' he murmured softly, looking down into her distressed face, his blue eyes smiling.

'She'll be fine shortly,' the doctor told Julian, gathering his things and preparing to leave as soon as he had given the injection.

'You'd better stay!' Julian said sharply, but the doctor shook his head.

'Not necessary. You've been this bad before?' he asked Merissa.

'W-worse,' she managed, and he nodded in satisfaction.

'She'll begin to pull round after a few minutes, but the itching will be a problem. Don't let her damage herself by scratching at her skin. She'll be sleepy soon with the injection. Right as rain tomorrow.' The doctor strolled off, stopping for a quick word with Mrs Patterson, who was hovering in the hall in her dressing-gown, and Merissa could feel irritation in Julian that only made her feel more miserable and unsafe.

'Can I do anything at all, Mr Forrest?' The housekeeper looked round the door and Merissa realised she was still being held securely in Julian's arms. Her face couldn't get any more red, though.

'No, you get back to bed. She'll be all right soon.' He stood for a minute and then lifted Merissa as if she was a child. 'Let's get you to bed too,' he said tightly, carrying her from the room and up the stairs. She wanted to tell him she could walk, but she wasn't too sure, and in any case he wouldn't have even answered, she was sure of that.

'I—I can see to m-myself,' she got out when he seemed to be about to prepare her for bed, and he let her go after a doubtful and frowning look at her.

'I'll get you a drink. I'll be back in a minute, so hurry up. What do you want—milk?'

'Water.' Merissa was already thirsty and she didn't fancy milk in the slightest.

She was already sitting up in bed when he came back, a glass of water in his hand, his jacket and tie discarded, and he switched off the overhead lights as he passed the switch, leaving the room softly lamplit.

She was grateful for the cool drink, but almost immediately went back to her obsessive scratching around her neck and face, even forgetting Julian's presence in her uncomfortable and painful ritual.

'Ah well,' he looked down at her before putting the glass on the table beside the bed and pulling off his shoes, 'I can't see any alternative.' He lay down beside her, his arms capturing her as he pulled her back against the pillows.

'W-what are y-you doing?' she gasped, panicking at once.

'Following the doctor's orders,' he explained, his hand trapping both of hers, making any movement impossible. 'I don't want you to look as if you've been in a fight tomorrow. You're costing me too much for me to allow you to damage yourself!'

Clearly the matter was decided, and for a minute Merissa lay still, biting her lip in an attempt to stop the irritation from driving her mad. Julian seemed to know her problem because his free hand began to stroke her face and neck, finding all the places that were driving her into the feeling that she would have to fight free and get up from the bed.

'Stick it out, there's a good girl,' he said quietly. 'It's bound to start working soon and then you'll be able to sleep.' She nodded against his shoulder—there seemed to be little else she could do—and his hand continued to soothe her.

'You're a real nuisance, aren't you?' he asked with quiet amusement, and it seemed like a good idea to simply nod again.

After a while she realised that the itching had stopped. The injection was working fast and she was sleepy already.

'I'm all right,' she whispered. 'It's stopped. You can let me go now, thank you.'

'Let's give it a while longer,' he muttered, sounding sleepy himself. 'Let's wait, just in case.'

'In case what?' she asked, yawning and trying to look up at him.

'In case you're never so sweetly willing to be here with me again,' he remarked, settling himself more comfortably on top of the bedclothes and tightening his arm around her.

Merissa suddenly found herself smiling and made no further move to free herself. For years, it seemed, she had been the one to take all the responsibility, the one to shoulder the load and face the problems, and it was good to be able to relax and forget everything. There was an almost frightening strength about Julian. Any woman he chose would never have to face problems. His wife would be cradled against any kind of worry and adversity. Even now, with her, he was placing her interests first, and it dawned on her sleepy mind that she loved him. If she had been fully awake she would have fought the very idea of it, but oddly enough, with her senses numbed by the injection and her body at last peaceful, the thought only brought her happiness and a feeling of safety.

She tried to hold on to the thought and the elusive feeling, because the morning would have to be faced and there was no future in such thoughts anyway. For now, though, there was no harm in luxuriating in the warmth of him and in the surge of joy that the unlikely dream brought. She made a small almost childlike sound of contentment in her throat, and Julian turned his head to brush her hair with his lips.

'Very likely,' he murmured, sleepily amused. 'Go to sleep, child.'

It was morning before she stirred, her face puzzled even before she opened her eyes. She knew something was different, but she wasn't sure at all what it was. The difference was inside her, in her mind, and she opened her eyes slowly as memory took the place of dreams and she recalled the small but frightening confession she had made to herself just before she had slept.

In the light of day she refused to accept it. To be in love with Julian Forrest was the biggest disaster that could have overtaken her. By his own admission he was ruthless in the way he despatched unwanted females from his busy life and Merissa had no illusions about his admission that he wanted her. Undoubtedly she was not the first and would not be the last. One thing was certain, however—she would leave his life as she had entered it; she was not going to have an affair with him, no matter how she felt.

The brief tap on the door had her stiffening with fright, hastily trying to remove from her face any lingering signs of her new vulnerability, and she was watching the door with an almost terrified look when Julian walked in.

'Awake?' he asked with raised eyebrows. 'Has the injection left you unable to speak? I had to take the chance on walking in. Perhaps next time you could make some sort of noise?'

'I've only just this minute opened my eyes,' Merissa muttered defensively, wondering what sort of a mess she looked lying there after her night's ordeal.

'Do you feel up to keeping to the schedule?' Julian asked briefly. 'Today you were to be introduced to your in-laws of the future.'

'I'm perfectly all right, thank you,' she managed. There was a hard look about him this morning that worried her, and she wondered when he had gone to his own bed and left her sleeping. He looked very strained.

'I'm sorry about last night,' she ventured. With the white pillows behind her she looked defenceless and unknowingly wistful. 'It doesn't often catch me out like that. Normally I can recognise even the slightest bit of it, like a sniffer dog, I suppose. I think the excitement must have dulled my senses. You must have had a very short night's sleep. I'm sorry.'

Julian was clearly unwilling to leave the doorway and come further into the room, his eyes guarded and cool, and she wondered why he was so annoyed when last night he had been so very good to her.

'Never mind,' he said shortly. 'I expected to have to look after you when I took you on. A little lost sleep is nothing to worry about. In any case, had it not been for the unfortunate incident I expect we would have stayed out very late. We probably had an earlier night than we would have done.'

Then why did he look so drawn and tired? she thought anxiously. This morning he was as distant as if he didn't know her at all, and she was well aware that her traitorous eyes were wanting to feast on him, to remember every look about him for the time when she would never see him again.

'Well, if you're sure you feel well enough, we'll stick to the plan and leave in about two hours. Can you be ready?' She nodded and he turned away abruptly. 'I'll have you something sent up for your breakfast,' he said tersely. 'This morning I prefer to eat alone. I have things to do.'

It was not any use arguing, she could tell that—and in any case she didn't want to. He had made his position clear. He wanted her to be as distant as possible. She had been settled in and now she was working, doing the job she was being paid to do. With a trembling sigh she left her bed and went to shower as soon as Julian had left, and when she came out, her breakfast was already there, a lonely little meal on her table. The lovely room looked dull suddenly, almost like a prison.

Julian was still distant and silent as they drove along in the sunlight of the late morning. He had made no comment about her clothes and she had tried not to annoy him any way. She had some very nice clothes of her own and even though they were not new, they had been chosen with care and suited her well.

This morning she wore a very pale coffee-coloured suit that showed off her tan and added deeper colour to her hair, her blouse a brown floral design. She looked demure and quiet, but he had an air of displeasure about him all the same, and she sat as quietly as she could, praying that he would recover before they reached his parents' home. She felt battered now that her new self-knowledge had sunk in, and she was in any case still sleepy from the effects of the injection, although she had told him she was fine.

'There it is,' he suddenly growled reluctantly. 'Charlwood Hall—my parents' home.'

Merissa could see it across the fields and she could see too that the road wound round to come close to the stone pillars of the gates. It looked about five-hundred years old, imposing and ivy-covered, with a village close by and an old church across the fields. Panic gripped her and she swallowed hastily.

'It—it looks very old . . .' she said weakly, surprised by Julian's quick laugh.

'Thank you. I built it ten years ago.' His lips twisted in wry amusement at her gasp of disbelief. 'My mother had a hankering for the ancient, my father has no liking for dust and crumbling woodwork, being a surgeon. We came up with a compromise. I don't normally confess to doing this kind of thing, but I don't want your dark eyes starting from your head should my mother tell you proudly that the old family residence is in fact as modern inside as a block of flats, because I designed it. One day, I imagine, it will be listed as a folly. For the moment, I keep quiet about it. I have no wish to be pressed to do anything like it again.'

'Don't you like working on things like houses?' asked Merissa shyly, half afraid and half happy that he had stopped the car so that she could look at the house from this distance.

'I prefer to work on a large scale,' he said briefly, his eyes on the beautiful house across the fields. 'I don't like to copy things either, but my mother wanted this, so . . .'

'What sort of a surgeon is your father? Maybe I ought to know, if this is to seem real.'

'Yes, I should have told you something more about them, I suppose, but somehow I never got around to it.' She could understand that because she knew that if it had not been for the involvement with Felicity she would never have met his parents. He would have wanted to keep her well away from them—in fact, it had occurred to her that they might not even know about the engagement party just in case she had not been up to the standard required in his life.

'My father works with sick children,' Julian was saying when she pulled herself back into the present and pushed last night's débâcle behind her. 'You're very pale, Merissa. I'm not at all sure we should have come.'

'We can go back, if you think I'll make a mess of things,' she said quietly, 'although I'll really try my best. I don't suppose you feel very rested yourself. I—I don't know what time you went back to—to . . .'

'I went back to my own bed as soon as you were deeply asleep,' said Julian abruptly.

'I—I well, it was very uncomfortable for you, I know, and . . .'

'Stop it, for God's sake!' he burst out roughly. 'I went back because I was too damned comfortable with my arm round you and you were altogether too vulnerable. The sleeping I didn't do was in my own bed. I'm not altogether a swine, although I did ponder on the idea of lying there until you surfaced and taking it from there!'

Merissa's cheeks flushed wildly and she turned her head away from him, only to annoy him further.

'Don't do that!' he rasped, turning her face back to his with rough insistence. 'You didn't want me to stay, did you?' he added with a sudden relapse into his soft and smoky tones. 'An affair with me isn't your idea of delight, is it?'

She shook her silky head, still avoiding his intent eyes, and his breath left him in a deep sigh as he grasped her shoulders and brought her closer. He just went on holding her until she looked up into his eyes, unable then to look away as she saw his own eyes darkening.

'You're a great blow to my pride,' he confessed softly. 'I almost feel like begging. It's not me at all. You don't even like me, and here I am like a hot-blooded youth, thinking almost all the time about ...'

'Please, Julian!' she interrupted anxiously, her hand out as if to ward off evil. 'Don't! You can make me do almost anything!'

'If I could believe that,' he said thickly, 'this trip would be cancelled right now.' Slowly and inexorably he was pulling her towards him until his eyes became her whole world. 'You look so innocent, so bewildered, Merissa. The sort of life you've led, the way you react to me—there must have been other men. What makes me so different that you don't want to live with me?'

No matter what she said he would never think well of her, she knew, and there was no point in sitting back and beginning an explanation of her life. Somewhere now there would be the realisation that she felt deeply about him, and that would be the end of her. He was too clever to fool completely. Let him remember Hugh and the things he had thought when he first saw her. He was puzzled now about her, but it was only because she had resisted him. Should that go then he would begin to think deeply about her, and then she was lost.

'I think we should go on,' she said anxiously, turning her face from him, and he let her go with a sigh.

'You're right, of course. I suppose we'll never get on with each other. Perhaps it was a mistake in the first place and I imagine I deserve all this, trapping you into doing something you had no desire to do.' He started the car and pulled out into the road. 'One thing good has come from it, however. Your mother is safely housed.'

'You chose the wrong person for the job,' said Merissa in a small voice. 'I'm grateful, though, for all you've done for my mother, it's just that you should have chosen somebody

else for the job. We don't really get on with each other at all,
which makes the pretending all that much more difficult,
and now you've got me cluttering up your life.'

'Maybe I don't mind you cluttering up my life at all,'
Julian said tightly. 'Anyway, it's far too late to have regrets.
Here we are.'

They had stopped in front of the beautiful old house, and
she realised that she had seen nothing of the driveway and
the gardens in her misery. She had no time to stand and
look around, though, because even before they had got out
of the car, Julian's parents were there to greet them and she
had another shock, another mystery. They were clearly
delighted, greeting her as if she was a longed-for daughter-
in-law, neither of them noticing, apparently, the hard and
tight look on Julian's face nor the worry on Merissa's.

Julian's father was as tall as his son, a big handsome man
with a face that had none of Julian's derision. She could
well imagine that he worked with sick children and also
that he suffered with them. They probably worshipped
him, she decided. He looked to be that kind of a man.

His mother was pretty, small and happy-looking, and
there was a contentment about her that Merissa knew
would be about her if she was married to Julian. There was
a great deal of love in this house, and she could well imagine
that Julian cared very deeply indeed for his parents.

'Come inside, dear,' his mother smiled, leading the way.
'We've heard so much about you, and you're every bit as
beautiful as Julian said.'

'Stop giving away my secrets!' ordered Julian in playful
anger. He took Merissa's hand, and she was grateful for
that. She knew that she was trembling and that he must feel
it. This was not the cool reception she had imagined, and
she could only think that he had misunderstood their
feelings for Felicity if they could greet her with such
enthusiasm. Certainly there was no coldness in them, and
she could not imagine they were the sort of people who
could put on this warmth for her benefit no matter how
good their manners.

'Come in and have coffee,' his mother invited happily, and as they went forward into the lovely beamed drawing-room, Julian's arm came firmly around Merissa's waist. Her nerves were so pent up that she almost jumped out of her skin—something that the keen dark eyes of his father did not miss.

'Look at the state he's got her into, Alice,' he remarked drily. 'Wouldn't you just know it? Time you were married, my lad, and settled into a nice groove like the rest of us!'

'Let the poor child get her foot in the door before she has to suffer your ribald humour! We get enough of that—but then we're used to it,' Julian's mother said firmly. 'If you can't behave yourself, Edward, then you'll have to have your coffee in the study!'

Merissa suddenly realised that she was in a family, a family who loved each other deeply, and her own misery deepened as she felt her deceit and unsuitableness more than ever. Gradually, though, in their company, her pent-up emotions eased and she felt on secure ground, more secure ground than she had felt since her father's death and since Julian had come so explosively into her life.

'What a pity Felicity isn't here today,' said Julian's mother during a break in the conversation, and Merissa felt Julian stiffen beside her. She was glad to feel his arm that had been lying along the back of the settee come tightly around her shoulders.

'I imagined she was still staying here?' he said, quietly casual.

'She's gone home, but she'll be back for the weekend, of course. You'll bring Merissa for the festivities, won't you, Julian?' his mother enquired.

'Naturally, but we can't stay long today. Merissa was ill last night and she's still a bit under the weather.'

They had to hear all about the allergy then and got off the subject of Felicity. It was impossible not to admire the smooth way that Julian could turn things to his advantage, but at least it gave Merissa breathing space, and after lunch as they walked in the gardens she found she was enjoying it all very much.

She loved to hear the quiet bantering that went on between Julian and his father, and she could see he was speaking only the truth when he had said he was very fond of his parents. What puzzled her was their attitude to herself. They were happy to see her and there was no stiffness in their attitude at all. She was not unaware that she had been closely observed, and whatever they had decided about her it was certainly not disapproval that showed on their faces. What about Felicity, then? The puzzles deepened daily, and she felt too tired to delve deeper right now, being only too ready to agree when Julian said they must go.

'Well,' he said quietly as they drove back to Creswell House, 'that wasn't so bad, was it?'

'They're very nice,' Merissa said with equal quiet. 'I liked them very much and I hate the idea of deceiving them. I don't like it any more than I like deceiving my own mother.'

'We could solve that easily enough,' Julian said softly.

'I don't see how,' she snapped, turning to him crossly, loving him and angry with him for her own pain.

'It's easy enough,' he assured her in a restrained voice, 'Let's make this engagement real.'

'You've got to be joking!' she gasped, staring at his tight face. 'I don't think, either, that this is the time for such jokes, even though you have a cruel delight in things like that.'

'I wasn't aware of being cruel to you, Merissa,' said Julian harshly. 'I'm not joking either. It's time I married and settled down to raising a family. I know it's what my parents want, and they seemed to be happy enough with you.'

'What about Felicity?' she asked with a sweet malice in her voice. The burst of joy she had felt at his unexpected proposal sank into deep unhappiness as she came to her senses rapidly and realised just who it was making such a proposal. Julian wanted her. He did not love her, and he would go right on with his life as if she did not exist after the flush of desire had faded.

'I've told you I want Felicity out of my life,' he said sharply. 'I think you know too that I want you *in* my life. You don't want deceit, and I can't say that it pleases me too much. I can give you anything you want. I can take care of your mother, take care of you, and we're not at all physically immune to each other. Good marriages have started with a worse base than we have.'

'No!' Merissa said loudly, then bit her lip anxiously. Her raised voice had been her attempt to push aside the little devil in her head that had urged her to accept, to take this little happiness that was offered. 'I—I'm sorry, Julian, but it's not possible.'

'Why?' he demanded harshly. 'Why isn't it possible? Goddard?'

'I've told you no on that score,' she said, trying to keep her voice calm and even. 'My mother and father were in love. It's clear too that your mother and father love each other deeply. That's the basis for a good marriage, and nothing else.'

'And of course you don't love me even one tiny little bit?' queried Julian in a hard voice, his eyes on the long road ahead.

'No. I've never pretended even to like you. This is a job, as you've pointed out to me several times. I'm grateful for your kindness to my mother and—and I'm grateful to you for being so nice when I wasn't well. If at any time I can do anything to repay you I will, but . . .'

'But you think that going so far as to stay engaged to me, to marry me is asking a bit too much?' he finished for her in a hard voice.

'Yes.' There was nothing else to say, and she hoped he wouldn't say anything either, because she was very close to weeping.

'Then, unfortunately, the deception continues,' said Julian with a flat finality. 'The job goes on until it's finished to my satisfaction.'

There was nothing left to say, and they were both silent and tense as they arrived back at Creswell House.

The post had arrived late and there was a letter from Clare, unusual in itself because Merissa had never told Clare that she was living here. But she forgot the mystery in her excitement.

'I've got a session with Derrick Lean!' she gasped with real pleasure, forgetting for the moment that she and Julian were not now on speaking terms.

His face reminded her. He looked thunderous.

'It's tomorrow,' she told him, a little subdued now. He would probably not let her go. 'Can I do the job?' She knew it sounded almost like pleading, but she really wanted to go. She had to know that there would be something left for her after Julian went out of her life. It was not now only the money. She wanted to work hard and get her life finally sorted out, then get away from any place where she could even be vaguely expected to see him.

'I don't break promises,' Julian said stonily. 'We agreed that you could go, and I can't see any reason why not.' He glared at her furiously. 'I can well do without that pleading little act too. Let's try to remember that you're a girl who can take care of herself in any circumstances, shall we?' He turned away, and Merissa felt deflated and miserable, her expression still not guarded as he suddenly turned back. 'What about that ramshackle car you drive?' he demanded in an irritated voice. 'You're too valuable at the moment to have you either involved in an accident or picked up by the police for driving something that's a public menace?'

'Well, I—I can't do anything about that between now and tomorrow, can I?' she asked weakly, his driving anger making her legs tremble. 'I'll only take it to the edge of London and then I'll park it and take the train.'

He nodded in a very grudging manner, his eyes skimming her face.

'All right. I'll get you another one as soon as I can get around to it.'

'Really, there's no need . . .' she began, but he turned

furiously away and stormed to the door, glancing back at her with brilliantly blue eyes, angry eyes.

'I'll decide whether or not there's a need!' he bit out. 'You just get on with your affairs—whatever they are!' The slamming of the front door made her jump, even though she was looking at it and expecting it.

'Oh, Mr Forrest went out?' Mrs Patterson appeared in the hall, looking worried.

'You could say that,' Merissa remarked with a deep sigh, worried herself.

'Oh dear, and I wanted to see him.' Mrs Patterson bit her lower lip anxiously. 'I've just got to have a few days off, Miss Troy. My sister's really ill and her husband is worked off his feet as it is. I want to go there and help out until she feels a bit better. I wanted to go now. Oh, dear!'

She looked really upset, and Merissa did not hesitate a moment.

'Well then, off you go, Mrs Patterson! I'll tell Mr Forrest when he gets back.'

'But what about the dinner, and what about getting his permission?' There was hope but also a trace of uneasiness in her face, but Merissa waved it aside.

'I can cook, for one thing, and for another, this house is immaculate. We can manage without anything being done for several days, I know. I'll tell him, don't worry—after all, I'm his fiancée!' She managed to put a great deal of reassuring confidence in her voice, and Mrs Patterson's face brightened.

'I've done the vegetables for tonight already. If you're sure it will be all right?' She turned at the kitchen door. 'You are a dear, Miss Troy.'

'Among other things,' Merissa thought with a resigned smile, mentally adding up her definite disadvantages according to Julian. He was not going to take too kindly to this act. She had taken it upon herself to be the mistress of the house, and no doubt he would have a great deal to say, none of it pleasant. Still, it was all she could do. She went up to her room to put in a bit of preparation for the next day's session with Derrick Lean, and in a very short while she heard the door slam again. Mrs Patterson had left and she had the house to herself.

She began to work furiously on her face and hands, refusing to think another straight thought, willing her mind to ignore Julian and his anger, his proposal of marriage, his desire for her. She knew it was that desire that was constantly making him edgy and annoyed. It seemed it took men like that. It merely made her unhappy. What a situation she had managed to get herself into! Yet there had never been any way out of it. She was trapped until Julian decided that the whole business could end.

She had a long, relaxing bath and washed and dried her hair, putting on a silky blue dress with a wrapover bodice and skirt, secured with a silver belt that held it snugly around her slender figure. It at least made her feel better and more able to face Julian and his wrath. She hurried down to the kitchen, suddenly realising that it was all up to her and that he would surely soon be back—not that she was certain of that at all, but she wasn't about to be caught off guard.

It was a lovely modern kitchen, everything there to work with, and she soon found herself doing what she loved to do, cooking, moving briskly around and humming softly as she prepared the rest of the meal.

The door bell startled her for a minute, but she thought that perhaps Julian, in his annoyance when he had gone, had forgotten his keys. When she answered the door, her face tightened with annoyance that she quickly hid. It was Louise Atherton, her face smiling and waspish, trouble written all over her expression.

'Julian's out!' Merissa had snapped the words out before she thought.

'Really? You do know, then, that I came here to see him? That's a relief, anyway. It saves me the trouble of having to convince you. I'll come in, if you don't mind,' Louise added, walking past Merissa and into the hall. 'As a matter of fact, I came to see you, not Julian, so if he's out then that's all to the good. It saves making pointless conversation until I can get you alone.'

CHAPTER SEVEN

THERE was a great deal of resolution in the voice that Merissa heard, and she closed the door after Louise with a resignation of her own. Julian was not here and she would have to cope with this all by herself.

Louise Atherton's attitude spelled trouble. It should have been quite clear from the very first that she was not the type to take this easily and simply go away very nicely. She was not about to give up Julian, and she clearly thought she had every right to be here. The realisation of this made Merissa unhappy. The woman was at home in this house, sure of herself and sure too that if she had encountered Julian, she would not have been so very unwelcome.

'Would you like coffee?' Merissa stood in the hall and tried to look at ease.

'No! I haven't come here for a little light chatter and entertainment. Let's get straight down to business!'

Louise walked into the sitting-room and made herself comfortable, sitting down and crossing her elegant legs, her eyes hard and uncompromising. Merissa was glad she had spent so much time on her appearance—at least she felt able to hold her own better when she looked good.

'There's something very wrong here—I can feel it,' Louise began in a hard voice. 'In the first place, you're not Julian's type at all, and in the second place, this great romance is altogether too sudden.'

'You seem to be in possession of a lot of information,' Merissa said quietly. 'Surely you know that men don't ever marry the type they're prepared to have brief affairs with!'

The shot hit home, but Louise Atherton was not too dismayed.

'Well, I'm glad you realise there is an affair between Julian and me,' she said vehemently. 'And it isn't going to just go away either. What I'm really interested in, though, is you. Julian is up to something, and I think I've just begun to get to the edge of it. You are the daughter of John Troy!' She smiled in a satisfied manner when the words had the desired effect. 'Julian was one of his students and then one of his greatest admirers. So it seems to me that he's doing this to get you out of trouble and get your mother into better circumstances. I know all about the great scandal, and I know now that you and John Troy's widow have been living in a great deal of poverty for ages. It's not at all typical of Julian, this gallant self-sacrifice, but I'd bet my bottom dollar I've hit the mark?'

'You'd lose your bottom dollar, Miss Atherton,' Merissa said sweetly, fighting down the trembling that this brought on. 'Julian and I are really engaged and we're really getting married. If you'd been right, then surely you have enough intelligence to realise that all he had to do was seek us out and offer a loan?'

'Oh, I've thought of that!' Louise said smugly. 'You see, I've not said I've got to the bottom of it, only that I've reached the edge of it. There's something more—something deeper. Quite obviously it's true that you're staying here, but not sleeping in that little bed that Julian spoke of so romantically—that's not him at all.'

Swinging one slender foot, her eyes keenly on Merissa's face, she watched for any sign of a crack in the smoothly beautiful face that was now flushed and anxious.

'What makes you think that?' asked Merissa. 'You seem to be telling me he had an affair with you—why don't you think it possible that he wants me? We are, after all, soon to be married.'

'You're too young and too unsophisticated for him!'

'Hasn't it ever occurred to you that I might also be pregnant? I mean, being so young and unsophisticated . . .' Merissa threw this in a little wildly, and was astounded at the effect.

'You lying little . . .' Louise sprang up and glared down at her. 'You can't be!'

'We've been in love for years,' said Merissa, standing too and facing the now white-faced woman. 'You obviously know he knew my father. We—we've been seeing each other for simply—ages,' she finished rather lamely. Louise, though, did not seem to notice Merissa's lack of conviction, she was too wildly angry, too consumed with rage. She simply turned and stormed out, opening the front door for herself and slamming out. Seconds later, her car left the front of the house in a great roaring of engine and a great squealing of tyres, and Merissa sank back into her seat, shaking all over and trying to consider what Julian would say if he ever managed to get hold of this information. He would not laugh it off, even if it had succeeded in getting Louise Atherton out of his life. Even that was by no means assured.

'Oh lord!' Merissa put her head in her hands and tried to get herself under control.

Finally she decided that she would have to think of some way to soften him up, and a good meal seemed to be the first step. She hurried to the kitchen and went on with the preparations for dinner. She made potato salad and a crisp green salad to accompany a quiche, and while this was in the oven she hurried across to the small and cosy sitting-room, preparing it with the sort of stealth that was usually reserved for Father Christmas, lighting a fire in the small fireplace and pulling the round table to the centre of the room. She drew the curtains on the now fading day and stood back to survey her handiwork. She had found a lace tablecloth and two pink candles, the room was pleasantly lamplit, and by the time Julian arrived, the fire would be a bright warming glow—if he came; she had no certainty of that. He had been in a very bad mood when he left.

He arrived just as Merissa was thinking about taking the quiche from the oven, and she hurried into the hall, anxiety written all over her face as she stood with nervously twisting hands and faced him in the hall's subdued lighting.

'Mrs Patterson's sister is very ill and her brother-in-law's really worked off his feet and she simply had to get away immediately, so I said it would be all right as I could cook the dinner, and I gave her permission—and I've cooked the meal . . .' Her voice trailed away into breathlessness, and Julian stopped in surprise, the rather grim look that had been on his face when he had come in fading into slightly bemused and wry amusement.

'Fine.' He said nothing else but continued to stare at her, his blue eyes narrowed and glittering. Merissa felt doubly anxious that he simply took it all in his stride and appeared to dismiss everything as perfectly normal.

'I—I don't know what's really wrong with her sister,' she went on, her face flushed. 'I forgot to ask, but anyway I don't suppose she would have wanted to tell me. I mean, it's really none of my business, is it? She might tell you, though, when she gets back, but I don't know when she'll be back . . . I told her that we—that I could manage . . .'

'Very good.' Still Julian hadn't moved, and Merissa stood there feeling foolish and very vulnerable, her slender figure looking almost breakable in the light of the hall, her hands still rather desperately twisting together.

'I—er—it's almost ready, the dinner, I mean.' He nodded and walked forward, but she backed away very rapidly towards the kitchen. 'You stay there, or somewhere, I'll tell you when it's ready . . .'

She fled to the kitchen, and he obviously gave up the idea of following, because she heard him go into the study and breathed a sigh of relief. She felt utterly foolish and so breathless that her hands were shaking in an alarming manner.

It took all her self-control to call him for the meal when she had it on the table and the pink candles lit, and even then she disappeared back into the kitchen to put the dessert into the oven, putting off the moment when she would have to face him again until the last possible minute.

He was standing puzzled in the hall when she went out, his hand on the dining-room door.

'It's a game,' he said with no expression on his face. 'Find the dinner. Are there clues dotted about the house?'

'Oh—it's in here.' She indicated the small sitting-room, blushing deeply at Julian's raised eyebrows as he came to the door and peered inside. Now that she could see it in its finished perfection, she thought less of the idea. The room was glowing with firelight and the light from the two bright pink candles. It looked very intimate and suggestive, and she switched on the overhead light to harden the scene, turning then and feeling dismayed as Julian walked out of the room.

He was back in seconds, however, with a bottle of white wine, and as he passed the switch, he switched of the rather glaring lights and plunged the room back into the warm glow of the lamps, the fire and the candles.

'Shame to spoil the effect,' he explained, holding her chair and bowing her into it. 'Let's hope the meal tastes as good as the room looks.' He sat opposite and poured the wine, there was nothing on his face to indicate that he was laughing at her, and Merissa breathed a little more easily.

When he had come in she had just caught a glimpse of something on his face that had really frightened her. It had been a deep anger. She knew they had parted on nothing like good terms, but Julian had then been merely displeased. Her initial glimpse of him in the hall, before she had drowned him with her rush of words, had shown more than displeasure on his face, and also something that had looked very like despair.

Merissa watched him pour the wine into his glass and sip a little, and she felt her heart leap at the sight of him so close to her, the handsome face so composed now, his hand steady as he held the wine bottle.

'I—I don't really . . .' she said quickly as he reached across to fill her glass, but he looked up at her with an odd little smile.

'One little glass to join me?' he coaxed. 'I promise not to try to make you drink more.'

'OK.' She served up the meal, feeling ridiculously shy,

unable to meet his eyes and very grateful when he started talking about his job. This effort to make the room cosy, to soften him up, had really backfired on her and she was filled with a sadness that it was not real. To be here permanently, listening to Julian's deep voice with its smoky softness, just the two of them eating by candlelight in this room, was a dream she had created without knowing she was doing it, and now it was threatening to make her cry.

She felt she was holding her breath, treading almost sacred ground, and Julian knew without doubt that there was something different. He went on talking, telling her about his latest ideas, about the trouble the new shopping centre had caused, the problems, and she sat with her eyes intently on him until he stopped and looked at her quizzically.

'Going to tell me what's going on in that odd little head of yours?' he asked softly, making her jump back guiltily, embarrassingly aware that she had been gazing at him with wide open eyes, listening hard but only hearing a little, too intent on drinking in the very sight of him to give deep thought to his words.

'I—I'm just simply listening,' she said, looking hastily away. 'Go on, do, it's all very interesting.'

'Tell me if you're bored out of your mind and we'll talk about something else,' he said quietly, an amused indulgence in his voice that made her cheeks flush.

'I'm not bored at all,' she said quickly. 'I—I was just thinking . . . aren't you a bit young to be so widely famous?'

'Luck,' he said briefly. 'Luck and your father.'

'My father?' Merissa's very fragile glow of happiness fled. Talk of her father invariably brought him back to thinking of her own inadequacies, and also of Hugh. But Julian went on with no change in his expression, and she gradually relaxed again as she listened to the beautiful voice and watched his face more secretly now.

'Did you know that I was a student of his?' he asked, not waiting for a reply but going on, 'The best thing that could have happened to me. He had an enormous influence on me. Without his help I would have been sent down after my first year.'

'You? Sent down!' Merissa stared at him, and he grinned attractively.

'Thank you for the vote of confidence,' he said mockingly. 'Actually I was a real tearaway and deserved to be kicked out. I was in and out of trouble from the moment I got there, and finally I went too far. It was only because of your father that I kept my place, and even he had to do some very fast talking on my behalf.'

'Whatever did you do?' she asked, her fork half-way to her mouth.

'A very childish dare. Too much to drink, a lot of encouragement, and I attempted to destroy a college monument.' He suddenly laughed at her expression. 'Not a church—a tree.'

'A tree?'

He nodded, his eyes dancing with laughter. 'Every college, as you probably know, has something that has acquired reverence by some means or other. At your father's college, it was a tree.'

'In the middle of the quad! An old dead thing like a sore finger!' Merissa suddenly remembered her father taking her around the university and pointing it out when she was only very young.

'The very one! There's a legend about it, something very like the ravens at the Tower of London. If the tree finally dies, the college will suffer some great disaster. It nearly did. I set fire to the tree.'

'And you were going to be sent down for a little thing like that?'

'My dear Merissa, it wasn't a little thing! It blazed merrily, damned near set fire to the whole college!' Julian grinned ruefully. 'It wasn't only that. I had a whole list of offences to be taken into consideration, a long list.'

He had actually done something wrong in his polished and perfect life! It made Merissa feel more than love, it softened her towards him incredibly, her warmth showing in her eyes, and for a minute they sat without speaking, simply looking at each other, until Julian took a deep breath and continued steadily.

'To get back to your father,' he said softly. 'He went in to bat for me. He told them I was brilliant, verging on genius, and he offered to take full and complete responsibility for me. To my surprise, they agreed. They knew him better than I did.'

Merissa couldn't take her eyes off him. To her, her father had been nothing but gentle, even though determined, and she couldn't imagine how he had tamed someone like Julian.

Julian had probably never had such an attentive audience, and her rapt gaze seemed to suddenly amuse him, because he lost the slight look of embarrassment and went on more easily, a light in his eyes that fascinated her even more.

'When I went to see your father in his study I was mortifed by the way he tore into me. He was livid, and I learned a lot about myself in those few minutes. There wasn't a crime large or small that he hadn't noticed, and he laid the law down with a vengeance. From then on he breathed down my neck, piled work on to me on top of my normal work and forced me to realise that I was at university for other reasons than to lark about. I attended every lecture he gave, whether it was on my schedule or not, and I learned! In the end it paid off, as he'd clearly known it would. I became an obsessive worker and I began to realise I had talent. In the vacation he got jobs for me with his overseas contacts, mostly in the Middle East—and that,' he finished, 'brings us full circle. That's why I was successful at a relatively early age.'

'How?' demanded Merissa, her chin on her hand, her eyes intently on his face, seeing the fine bone structure thrown into relief by the firelight, seeing how the candle-light caught the blue of his eyes, the gleam of his hair.

'Well,' he continued slowly, his eyes searching her face, 'to complete the life story, I got to know the Middle East.

The oil states were just emerging into this century, they wanted to make a splash, as it were. Because of working there, I'd picked up a smattering of the language, found out the sort of thing they were after. There was a competition for the design of a new airport and hotel complex for one of the Gulf States and I won it in my first year out of university. It was a success. It made a name for me, and I came back and used a legacy from my grandfather to set up on my own. End of story, except that when your father died I was back there planning an extension for them. I didn't know about his death until I got back and by then it was too late, it was all over.'

'You didn't know my mother?' she asked, tears in her eyes as she thought about this new side to her father. She drew back into the shadows to hide her little burst of grief.

'No,' he said quietly. 'I knew the sort of person she was, she had plenty of young admirers among your father's students, but I never had the pleasure, I was working too hard. I met you, though.'

'Me?' Merissa forgot the tears as she looked at him in surprise. 'I don't remember you.'

'You were about eight at the time,' Julian laughed. 'Not quite the age to remember a serious and rather boring student. I saw you with your father one day, hanging on to his hand like a lifeline. I remember looking into two dark eyes, strange eyes, and seeing how shy you were. My desire to pat you on the head had to be curbed. I just knew you'd jump right into his pocket.'

'I used to be very shy,' Merissa said quietly, avoiding his eyes.

'I sometimes get the impression that you still are,' he told her. 'What's for afters?'

She pulled herself together, reaching for the plates, but he stood too.

'I'll take those.' His voice brooked no argument, and she brought the second course back as he stacked the plates in the dishwasher, coming back then to tuck into gooseberry tart and cream.

There was a silence now between them that worried her very much, and she searched around for a topic of conversation.

'I'm afraid it's not a balanced meal,' she said authoritatively. 'Two lots of pastry. It's not balanced.'

'So I can expect to be leaning sideways tomorow?' asked Julian, his eyes amused.

'Not unless you go on drinking!' she said with a rather severe look at the wine bottle, and he corked it firmly.

'Telling one's life story is very thirsty work,' he said softly. 'Why did you make this delicious tart if you disapprove of it?' he shot at her quickly, and she felt on very dangerous ground.

'I—well, I wanted everything to be a bit—er—comfortable. I had to tell you Mrs Patterson wasn't here, and I did take it upon myself to give her permission to go, and I didn't really have the right to do that.'

'No,' he agreed seriously, 'you didn't. You thought I'd be annoyed?'

'It did cross my mind.'

She had to watch her step with him now. She wanted to sit and look at him, talk to him, laugh with him, and she had to keep reminding herself that this was merely temporary, a job she had been tricked and bullied into. Her new feelings had to be kept hidden at all costs.

'That was really good.' Julian said with a contented sigh as he sat later on the settee, his legs stretched out in front of him, coffee on the table at his side. 'I feel well fed and sleepy. Pour me some more coffee,' he added lazily.

Merissa nearly told him to do it himself, but she was so pleased to see him happy and relaxed and she knew that sooner or later she was going to have to tell him Louise Atherton had been here, so she crossed to get his cup, reaching across him when he made no move to pass it to her. It was then that he grasped her wrist tightly, tugging her off balance and on to his lap.

'Julian!' Her cry of outrage did not in any way affect him,

and he grasped her chin, making it impossible to avoid his eyes.

'Now it's your turn to talk!' he said with none of the warmth that had been there during dinner. 'Tell me about Louise's visit.'

'You—you know?' Merissa forgot to struggle as she gazed up into two eyes as brilliant and hard as blue ice. 'How—how . . .'

'She was driving furiously along when she spotted my car coming this way,' he explained with a look of menace that she feared. 'She flashed the lights, blew her horn and damned near caused an accident reversing to get back to me. I then got the works, in no uncertain way!'

'Why—why didn't you tell me when you first came in, then, if you . . .'

'How could I?' he rasped. 'We were playing at house, weren't we? Mothers and fathers, husbands and wives.'

'We weren't!' Merissa struggled furiously, but he held her with very little effort and she subsided with as much grace as she could. 'She came here demanding to know if you were pretending this engagement so that you could help my mother and me. She knows who I am, and all about my father,' she added accusingly.

'Don't look at me,' he growled. 'I wouldn't give her the time of day, let alone tell her anything about John Troy's family. I could tell, though, that you got rid of her and settled that little idea.'

'Well—yes . . .'

'Well—yes,' Julian repeated angrily. 'So now perhaps you can tell me. I'd like to know all about this baby.'

'What baby?' In spite of the fact that she had blurted this untruth out to Louise, Merissa had forgotten it, and it was only when he snarled at her that she realised why he was so filled with rage.

'The one you're having,' he said with a sinister quiet, his grip tightening painfully.

'It's not true! You know it's not true! I said it to get rid of her!' She dared not struggle now, and he stared deeply into her eyes, seemingly intent on reading the truth, his breath leaving him in an audible sigh when her face seemed finally to convince him.

'You're weird,' he commented, the cruel grip relaxing. 'No girl goes around saying things like that. Why did you say it!'

'She was so sure of herself,' muttered Merissa, her face red. 'She kept on telling me she knew all about my father and our life and that you only wanted to do something for us because of our—our circumstances . . .'

'So you thought you'd give her another set of circumstances to ponder on?'

'I—I suppose so.' She was filled with embarrassment and no little fear. Julian had relaxed a bit, but he was by no means back to any kind of normality. She could feel tension in him that was spreading rapidly to her, tightening her breathing.

'You suppose so,' he mocked. 'She thinks this hypothetical baby is mine!'

'I know. I'm sorry . . . But really she'll soon find out that it's not true, won't she? I mean when—when . . .'

'Crazy!' he muttered, her breathless little plea finally convincing him completely. 'What about your reputation, then? What about mine, for that matter?'

'You didn't seem to care much about that when you told her about the very small bed that we shared!' she blurted out angrily, flushing at his amused and speculative look. 'You weren't thinking about anything then but getting rid of her!'

'Oh, but I was,' he drawled. 'I told you I was daydreaming, but the thought of you telling her you were pregnant naturally brought the thought of Goddard into my mind, and . . .'

He got no further. Merissa went into wild action, fighting and struggling, her face flaming with anger and embarrassment.

'I hate you! You think you can say anything to me. How dare you say that!'

'It's really strange,' Julian said softly, pulling her tightly against him and foiling her escape attempts. 'The mention of Goddard drives you into a rage in this particular instance—and yet you were quite prepared to allow a person like Louise to think I was responsible. If you want to indulge in a litle daydreaming yourself, I really don't mind. Tell me about it,' he finished softly, his lips trailing over her cheeks and along the edge of her jawline. 'Let's play at house again—I liked it. What do we do now dinner's over?'

'Please let me go,' she said shakily, fighting now to keep her lips from trembling.

'No!' His adamant and brief refusal widened her gaze and she looked quickly away as tears filled her eyes. 'Don't cry, darling,' he said softly, wiping the tears away. 'I want you. I want you to stay with me, sleep with me, make love with me. I want us to talk as we've done tonight, but this time I want it to be as we lie close together in the darkness.'

She looked at him wonderingly. His voice was gentle and deep, warm and sincere, and he brushed her lips with his, his eyes intent on her face.

'We've both enjoyed this evening,' he said with a certainty in his speech that she could only agree with. 'I don't want you to go back to Goddard or anyone else, because I can't bear to think of anyone else touching you but me.'

She wanted to tell him that nobody ever had done. In all her years she had never been on any man's lap except her father's, and nobody had ever kissed her as Julian had.

'You don't want to stay engaged to me and you don't want to marry me,' he continued urgently. 'All right, I won't make any attempt to tie you down. Live with me, stay here. It's long past the joking stage with me, Merissa. I can't keep my hands off you. I can't even try.'

He looked at her intently, drowning her in the blue depths of his gaze, holding her eyes with hypnotic ease. He lifted her hand to his mouth, his lips on the palm, moving softly, suddenly biting the soft mound at the base of her thumb and bringing a small inarticulate cry from her as his tongue soothed the place and his mouth pulled erotically at her skin. It was almost shocking, and her heart raced as her face flamed with colour.

'Don't!' She managed a cry of denial, but her head sank to his shoulder, her whole body weak and trembling, and his lips came to her neck, moving against the pulse that accelerated at his nearness.

'Touch me, Merissa!' he said huskily, placing her flat palm against his chest.

'No! I don't want to!' She shook her head in despair, moaning as kisses heated the skin of her neck and cheeks.

'You do!' Julian insisted thickly. 'Touch me, darling.' His hand guided her to the open neck of his shirt, his fingers flicking open buttons and drawing her hand intimately against the warm power of his chest, against his pounding heart. 'Don't move away,' he breathed against her lips.

She couldn't anyway. She was entranced, her fingers moving delicately against the warmth of his skin, lightly tensing in the crisp, dark covering of hair and he groaned softly.

'At last! At last, my beautiful Merissa!'

His mouth closed over hers, devastating her, and as if he knew she was powerless to move her fingers from the slow exploration of his skin, he in turn began to discover the warmth of her body.

'I can't sleep any more without you,' he muttered, his breathing heavy and deep as his mouth left hers to rest against her neck, his lips just touching her hot skin. He was breathing in the scent of her like an animal seeking home, and her pulses raced in her throat.

She was languid, in a dream, her eyelids heavy, arching as to an electric shock as his hand moved inside the wrapover dress to seek the swollen mound of her breast. She was caught up in the craving that was growing inside to a deep, sweet pain, and Julian pulled aside the silken blue of her dress to expose the golden silk of her breasts.

'Say you want me, Marissa!' he urged heatedly. 'Say you

want more than this! Tell me!

Unable to speak, she nodded her head, crying out as his mouth searched her breasts hotly, his hands moving the dress aside, tossing the silver belt to the floor and sliding the dress from her as she lay unresisting.

His hands were warm on the slender body he had uncovered, and then he took her head in both hands, cupping her face, looking deeply into her eyes, his own eyes dark with passion.

'You're perfection,' he muttered. 'Golden silk in my arms, slender and graceful. I've wanted you since I first saw you, wanted you as I've never wanted a woman before.'

'Louise!' she cried with soft bitterness, his words bringing her some way back to reality and to the knowledge that he did not love her and that Louise knew this house, had probably lived here, been in his arms in this room.

'What about her?' he murmured, kissing her deeply.

'You've had her here, made love to her . . .'

'No, my jealous little sweet,' he said softly, smiling down at her. 'She's been here with other guests, but never as anything other than a guest. She's got an erotic imagination.'

Allowing no further talk, he drew her beneath him, his body pressing her into the soft upholstery, his legs tangling with hers as he claimed her lips eagerly, forcing her against his muscled body, his mouth urgently and warmly invading hers.

Merissa was slowly sinking into pleasure, nothing else real but the demanding lips and hands, the hard urgent body, and her arms wound around his neck, drawing him closer, signalling submission.

The fierce and persistent ringing of the doorbell jerked her back to the reality of the quiet and warm room, and she stiffened in a moment of shock as she drifted upwards from her dreamy state.

'The doorbell!' she gasped, but he didn't seem to be able to hear either her or the bell. 'Julian!' He raised his head and looked at her with dark and dazed eyes, his pupils dilated, his lips reaching again for hers.

'They'll go away,' he groaned. 'They must. I want you so much!'

They didn't, though. The ringing continued with a sharp urgency that finally got through to him, and he sighed, looking at her ruefully.

'Saved by the bell!' he murmured wryly, his head swooping down to give her one last fierce kiss before he stood and straightened his shirt. 'Don't panic,' he added quietly as she struggled to sit up. 'Whoever it is, they won't be coming in here. If they have to stay, I'll use my study.'

He went out, closing the door behind him, but she heard his greeting when he opened the front door even so.

'Dick—you damned nuisance! What the devil do you want at this time of night?'

'Sorry, have I interrupted something?' Merissa heard the deep embarrassment in the voice and heard too Julian's quiet laugh.

'Nothing that won't keep. I'll just tell her I'm going to be busy. Go into the study.'

'Gosh, I'm sorry. I heard you'd got engaged. John Troy's daughter, isn't it?'

'That's right,' said Julian easily. 'It's as well to keep things in the family. Anyway, it keeps her out of mischief. Did you get copies of the site engineer's reports?'

'The lot!' The voice held an almost savage satisfaction and she heard Julian's answering triumph,

'Good, now we're almost there. All I need is that tape. Go in, I'll be right back.'

Merissa heard him crossing the hall and hurriedly fastened the silver belt, still pretending to be busy with the buckle as he came into the room. Obviously he had no idea that his conversation could be heard so clearly, and her mind was trying to make sense of his remarks. She was hurting from the flippant words he had used to the man at the door, hurting at the way he had recovered from what to her had been such a devastating experience, and her mind was now clear and cool.

'I'm sorry, Merissa,' he said, coming close and taking her by the shoulders. 'It's Dick Finley, and it's too important to be put off to another time.' She didn't answer, and he tilted her face to the light.

'I'm sorry,' he repeated, looking at her intently. 'I didn't mean to leave you high in the air.'

'I'm firmly on the ground,' she said, looking straight at him. 'I'm going to bed—I'd hate to look tired at my session with Derrick Lean tomorrow.'

'I don't know how long we'll be,' Julian said softly, his hands lingering on her face. 'Go to my bed, I'll wake you when I come up.'

'No, thank you,' she managed tightly, jerking her face away from his touch. 'I seem to remember that we've been through all this before, and if you recall, the answer was no. It's still no.'

'What's the matter with you?' He jerked her into his arms, his face beginning to show anger at her attitude. 'Minutes ago you were as deeply involved as I was. If I came for you, you'd be willing again within seconds, and we both know it!'

'I did confess that you can make me do almost anything,' Merissa managed coldly. 'You've certainly got a lot of experience, and you're altogether too much for my little experience. If that's the way you want it, then I can hardly stop you, can I?'

'It's not the way I want it, and you damned well know that! I'm not into seduction!'

'Then that's all there is to say,' Merissa told him quietly. 'Goodnight.'

Julian let her go and she walked out and up the stairs, undressing without even putting on the light and falling into bed after washing her face quickly. She could not afford to let herself think at all. Downstairs, she knew, Julian would have forgotten her existence. He would be studying reports, deeply interested in the visitor and talking over his plans. What tape? Did it concern her father? Had it anything to do with her father's tapes? Her mind refused to work. How could her father's music tapes be in any way connected with site engineers' reports? She fell into a deep but troubled sleep, her mind reeling between Julian and buildings, between her father and the lovely sound of some of the music he had collected that now seemed to be out of reach to anyone, except Julian.

CHAPTER EIGHT

AFTER the next day's photographic session, Merissa felt unable to simply turn around and go back to Creswell House. Yesterday had left her deeply depressed, and she wanted to avoid Julian. She was sure now that he would only have to take one look at her face and he would know she loved him. Her own actions and her ready surrender would have alerted him to the fact had he not been so sure deep down that she had been having an affair with Hugh. If he really knew the extent of her innocence he would not have to be so very clever to realise that her willingness with him stemmed from love and nothing else. It was merely now a matter of time before she was out of his life, and she knew she would have to fight to keep free of any further involvement with him.

She missed her mother very badly, and with very little thought she simply turned in the direction of the cottage when she had finished, risking life and limb in her old car over such a distance but needing to see someone who would never start to pull her apart.

Julian had been out when she had left in the morning, and she imagined he had completely forgotten about her assignment. From saying that her car was too dangerous to drive he had apparently been quite willing to see her bring it into London. So much for his concern! He had been more concerned when she had first come to Creswell House and had insisted on her driving behind him all the way so that she could have her own transport. He didn't care now.

It was really wonderful to see her mother, and she had to work very hard not to come out with the whole sorry story. The only thing that stopped her was the happiness on her mother's face and the concrete signs of improving health. If she told her, her mother would insist upon leaving at once—and why should she? Merissa argued. It was Julian's idea when he had made this impossible situation—the bonus. She held her tongue and tried to relax.

Her mother, though, was full of Julian. Apparently he was there frequently and had been there yesterday when Merissa had thought he was working somewhere. He had been going through her father's tapes, and her mother was quite convinced he was some sort of avid collector of the classics.

'Of course,' she said warmly, 'if he asks to borrow any of them, then I'll let him. I wouldn't for anyone else, but for Julian . . .'

For Julian! Yes, they were both under his spell in different ways. Merissa knew she was not even capable of thinking straight as far as Julian was concerned, and all her mother's miseries seemed to be dissolving at last, the tight and intent look on her face since her husband's death was easing, and Merissa would have felt the same if she had not now taken on an even greater burden with her love for Julian.

She lingered at the cottage for as long as possible, pushing the unease about her car and its lights into the back of her mind. She could relax here.

She was just about to go when the headlights of another car came sweeping up the drive, a fast and powerful car, and her heart gave a little leap of gladness mixed with fear. It could only be Julian, especially swinging in through the narrow gateposts like that.

He lashed out at her at once, mindless of the startled presence of her mother.

'Didn't you hear me the other day?' he grated. 'I said I

don't want you driving that car! It was nearly dark before it dawned on me that no photographer goes on that long. Luckily it dawned on me too that you'd probably be here, otherwise I'd now be doing the rounds of the hospitals or the police stations!'

'If you'd phoned . . .' Merissa began, but got no further.

'And have you driving off in that contraption?' he asked grimly. 'Catching you here seemed to be a much better idea.'

He suddenly seemed to become aware of Mrs Troy, but he made no move to cover up his anger.

'How have you managed to control your daughter for twenty-three years?' he rasped. 'Give me a few tips!'

'She's never been anything but good as gold,' her mother asserted, and to Merissa's astonishment, she was laughing. 'Of course, I couldn't do much about the car. I'm glad you came for her.'

Merissa was beginning to wonder if anyone at all was on her side, and her mother gave her a hug as Julian made it quite clear that it was time to go.

'It's wonderful to see how much he cares about you,' she whispered. 'Someone to take care of you at last, darling. It's like a dream come true. He was white with anxiety when he came in!'

White with anger, Merissa wanted to correct, but she kept it to herself. She could see the whole thing from Julian's point of view. She could even see the news item: 'Fiancée of Julian Forrest spends the night in a cell.' Of course, then the story of her father would come out too. Julian wouldn't want notoriety, even if he did believe in her father.

She settled glumly beside him as he put her firmly in his car and gave a half-hearted look at her own car standing there so shabbily outside the cottage.

'What's to become of it?' she murmured almost to herself.

'Tomorrow it goes to the nearest scrap yard!' he grated, his eyes on the dark road as they turned out of the drive and headed back to London.

'No! It's not yours to dispose of. I'll decide what to do with it. After the weekend I'll come back down and do something about it. I'll drive it to a garage and see if they can make something of it.'

'They can,' rasped Julian. 'They can make scrap metal.' He wound the window down and tossed something into the cold-looking waters of a stream they happened to be passing. 'Never leave your keys in a car,' he advised with a grim satisfaction. 'That car stays where it is until a breakdown truck tows it away.'

'How dare you throw my keys away?' stormed Merissa, realising just what he had done so arbitrarily.

'Somebody has to keep you in one piece,' he informed her with infuriating calm. 'For want of a keeper, that person is me. This week I'll get you another car.'

'Why should you?' she raged, her face flushed with annoyance. 'You've told me more than once that I'm being paid handsomely and the bonus is for my mother. I don't want any charity from you!'

'Oh, is that what it is?' he enquired with quiet sarcasm. 'Well then, let's say it's a bonus for the pleasure of holding you in my arms and feeling your explosive reaction to me.' He went on before she could get any word in. 'Why the hell didn't you take the Mercedes? I left it there in the garage right next to your incredible little heap. The keys were in the ignition and I took the bigger car.'

'How was I supposed to know that?' she asked, turning to look at his tight profile, her heart giving a little skip when she realised he had remembered after all.

'It should have been obvious!' he snapped. 'You know I like the smaller car in town. I thought you'd be able to manage it better than the big one, but of course, being you, you took the incredible heap out and scared me— deliberately!'

'I did not! If you'd wanted me to take the Mercedes you should have told me!'

'You were asleep when I left—at least I assumed that you were, and I wasn't about to come in and find out!' he rasped irritably. 'I had a bad night with almost no sleep. I wasn't in the mood to face you and your peculiarities.'

'It's hardly my fault you sat up half the night with your visitor!'

'He left quite quickly,' Julian said in a sort of low growl. 'I spent the night, or the greater part of it, pacing my own room and telling myself that coming in to get you would be very wrong.'

He suddenly swung off the road to a small hotel and had her out of the car before she could protest. She was still digesting this latest information and not at all ready to face him in the lighted dining-room.

'I—I could cook at home . . .' she began, but he gave her a wry look that silenced her.

'Really? Look where that got us last night,' he reminded her. 'I think we'll eat here—the food may be worse, but the after-effects will be better. I don't want another night with my stomach twisted in knots while you sleep in your bed and I walk round mine.'

Merissa sat silently after their order was taken, and he suddenly covered her hand with his.

'I know you want me, Merissa,' he said bitterly. 'So why are you doing this to us? There's a great deal of sheer joy waiting for us and you know it, yet you're prepared to serve out your time and then simply walk out of my life without ever knowing what it could be like. I'll give you anything you want.'

Except love, she thought miserably. She kept her eyes downcast, and he sighed and moved his hand, leaving her feeling cold and deserted.

'Oh, all right,' he said resignedly. 'I've never begged before for anything, let alone a woman. You have that distinction at least. If you imagine, though, that I'm going to let you go back to Goddard,' he added with a menace in his voice, 'then think again, my sweet.'

'I'm not going back to Hugh,' she whispered miserably.

'Oh? Set your sights higher, have you? Well, that's good news, I expect.'

They did not speak again, there being nothing now to say, and Merissa was pleased to leave when the rather uncomfortable meal was over. It seemed they would never now be able even to be civilised with each other.

The weekend seemed to stretch before her like a bad dream. Now, with the new situation between herself and Julian, she dared not relax in any way. If she showed any sign of either gentleness or friendliness he would think she was considering his suggestion, and indeed sometimes she was. Surely, her treacherous mind urged her, it would be better to agree to the reality of the engagement, to marry him and live without love, than never to see him again, or even worse, to see him with someone else. But she would have to face the thought of someone else anyway. It would be unbearable to belong to him and not have him belong to her.

He was silent, grimly and angrily silent, a silence that seemed to scream in her ears, and Felicity was there. She was a small and slender girl who watched Julian with sad eyes whenever she thought nobody else was looking. A girl who followed him about like a beaten dog.

Merissa liked her on sight, and she knew that this time she couldn't do the job she was being paid to do. Nothing would make her be nasty to this girl, or stand by while Julian made one of his remarks and back him up.

She told him this decision as she walked with him in the gardens, the only time that they had been alone together, because they had avoided each other whenever possible by an unspoken mutual agreement. He had been helping his father to prepare some kind of outdoor party that was to take place that evening, and now, in the morning sunlight of the day after their arrival, she firmly stated her intentions.

'I'm calling the bargain off,' she told him as they walked along in silence. 'I'll stay the weekend, but then I'm going away altogether, out of your life, out of this ridiculous situation.'

Julian spun her round to face him, instantly savage.

'And what makes you think I'll simply allow you to walk off as free as a bird?'

'You'll have to take whatever reprisals you think necessary,' she said quietly, her eyes on her toes. 'I can't be nasty to Felicity.'

'Why?' He lifted her chin, forcing her to meet his eyes. 'Why can't you stick it out with Felicity? She's only another Louise, and you handled *her* very well all by yourself.'

'She's not another Louise!' Merissa cried hotly. 'Louise is a nasty, vicious person, but Felicity . . .'

'Go on,' he encouraged quietly.

'She's different. She worships you. She doesn't deserve to be unhappy, and I can't hurt her any more—she's hurting enough as it is.'

'Maybe you'd better think of all the things you'll be losing when you walk out and then consider Felicity in the light of that!' he snapped, his hands becoming painful on her face.

'I've considered,' she stated as best she could, struggling uselessly. 'I'll have to tell my mother it was all a lie. I know she'll be hurt, but I know she wouldn't want me to hurt somebody simply to keep her cottage, her comfort.'

'Ever thought that you'll be hurting me by simply walking out of my life?' Julian asked quietly, his hands relaxing on her face. He moved his fingers into her hair, his thumbs probing her cheeks. 'I need you, Merissa!'

'If—if you're still going on about your suggestion,' she began tremulously, 'then I won't change my mind about that either.'

'I'll make you change your mind,' he said softly, locking his fingers behind her neck and pulling gently.

'You couldn't!' she said stiffly, resisting the temptation to move against him, her eyes looking anywhere but into the hypnotic blue of his.

'I will!' he breathed.

She was locked in his arms before she could move one inch away and his lips roamed hotly over her face and neck, his hands warmly possessive against her arched back as she struggled to be free.

'They'll see us from the house!' she gasped anxiously.

'Let them,' he growled. 'If they have any sense they'll assume we sleep together. If I had any sense they'd be right!'

'Felicity will . . .' Merissa began in a panic as his lips determinedly made their way to hers.

'Damn Felicity!' he rasped, tightening her to him. 'It's you I want, not Felicity. You're the one who winds herself around me, who fits me as if I'd fashioned you myself. I'll never have a moment's peace in my life until I take you!'

He drew her round the corner, out of the sight of the house, leaning against the fence and pulling her tightly into the hard cradle of his hips, his mouth covering hers with a desperate urgency, and as usual, Merissa relaxed against him with a low moan of despair. There was no way she could resist his arms, and he knew it.

'You belong to me!' he said possessively, pulling the shirt from her waistband with rough pleasure and sliding his hands on to the smooth warmth of her back. 'Every time I touch you, every time I hold you, I feel it. You say you don't want to stay engaged, don't want to marry me, but you want me—you're mine any time I ask you! I'm asking you, darling.'

His lips were drugging, deeply searching her mouth as her lips parted beneath his, and all thought of Felicity, her mother, her determination, fled at the magic.

'My beautiful, beautiful Merissa,' murmured Julian against her lips. The hands that had been stroking her back, urging her against him, were now at her breasts, his fingertips brushing the hardened peaks gently, making her moan with pain and pleasure, and there was now no need to hold her, her arms were tightly around him. 'You need this like a drug, don't you? Think what it will be like, darling, night after night in each other's arms, nothing to come between us.'

Mindlessly she was straining to get closer, heat flooding through her, all thoughts banished except the urgent and painful feelings that only he could bring and only he could assuage, and he crushed her close, his own desire very obvious and thrilling, his lips demanding and triumphant.

'Don't go, Merissa!' he groaned. 'I can't let you leave me. You know what there is between us. We've got to get this out of our systems!'

'And how long will that take?' she asked, her voice only a weak sound in her ears.

'Who can tell?' he murmured huskily. 'Right now it feels as if it will be forever, but maybe in a few months, a few years, we'll be just good friends, easy in each other's company. I won't tie you down, Merissa.'

Just good friends! Old companions with amusing anecdotes to exchange, shared memories. She loved him! To have nothing was better than that! She tore herself away and ran back to the house, tears streaming down her face.

'Merissa?' She looked up later from her lifeless contemplation of the cover of her bed to find Felicity standing in her doorway, her face unhappy. 'I'm sorry to come in uninvited, but—well, I heard you crying.'

'It's all right.' Merissa managed to smile, sitting up and pulling herself together rapidly. 'It's nothing really. Julian and I had a few sharp words, nothing to worry about.'

Even now she was covering up for him. She really ought to be telling Felicity the whole story, but she couldn't let him down.

'I don't think . . . I mean, don't take it too hard,' Felicity ventured. 'Julian can be a real pig, but he really cares about you. When you're not looking, the way he looks at you is beautiful.'

She seemed to be on the verge of tears herself, as she walked out without another word, and Merissa had to squash the impulse to run after her and tell her everything. Yes, Julian probably did look at her like that—when he was quite sure that Felicity was watching. He was cold-blooded and calculating, even if she did love him.

She didn't speak to him again, and also he avoided her, so that it was Julian's mother who told her about their festivities.

'Hasn't Julian told you?' she asked in exasperation. 'Oh, my dear, I hope you've brought some jeans and an old shirt. This is the day we entertain the children Edward has had under his wing during the year. Some of them are now healthy, some of them are poor little things who'll never be healthy, but they all come. There'll be about forty children, and we have a barbecue just as it's getting dark and then fireworks. Edward and Julian have been setting them up all the time you've been here. They're really very good at it, quite professional. Anyway,' she added, patting Merissa on the arm, 'they'll be here soon, and I should get changed if I were you. Children can be very sticky!'

She hurried off to get changed and Merissa followed, coming down later in the only jeans she had brought, white ones.

'I haven't any others,' she explained as Mrs Forrest shook her head worriedly.

Julian was just coming in, looking very businesslike in blue jeans and a dark sweater, and his eyes moved over Merissa with an angry deliberation.

'It's no use looking at her like that,' said his mother, mistaking his look for something quite different. 'She's only brought these, but I really think you could have told her. I expect they'll wash, but really!' she said accusingly. 'Oh, they're here!'

Everyone hurried out, the housekeeper and her husband as enthusiastic as any children and Felicity looking happy for once, definitely used to this, one of the family, even though Julian was determined that she shouldn't be. It made Merissa feel very much of a fraud and an outsider. She had no right whatever to be here.

'Merissa——' Julian began, having lingered behind, but she cut him short, her eyes looking through him.

'Please don't start again,' she asked quietly. 'I can't go on with this. After this weekend I leave. I'm just not capable of going on with this deceit, and the alternative is not any consideration at all, so please don't mention it again.'

She walked out on to the lawn and was there with the others when they waited to greet the children who got off the bus. Julian's father remembered them all, and Merissa forgot her own problems as she saw theirs. Between them they seemed to have so many physical disabilities, but they were so cheerful that she felt ashamed. Their excitement was infectious too, and she was kept busy helping to feed them and keep them all shepherded into a safe area as the darkness fell.

Julian's mother and father were tireless, and so was Julian. Obviously too he was quite used to having Felicity around, and they worked as a team so easily, frequently laughing together. Felicity belonged here and Julian had a great affection for her, Merissa could see that, and she could not understand at all why he wanted to get rid of her. Often he was beside her, his arm around her shoulders as she looked up at him with laughter on her face. Merissa was cut out altogether. When he was not near her he so rapidly forgot his desire. What price an engagement that was real, a marriage that was based on such a weak and passing emotion? It was this day-to-day loving, this companionship, that finally made a marriage work.

'I've never been here before,' a little voice piped up at her side, and Merissa looked down at a small girl who was clearly scared.

'Neither have I,' Merissa confessed with a smile, 'but there are fireworks soon.'

'I'll be frightened!' The little face puckered and Merissa bent down, lifting the pitifully frail little girl into her arms.

'I'll hold you if you like,' she soothed. 'They're only coloured lights—they're lovely. We'll watch them together.' The hands came firmly round her neck and she found herself laughing quietly. 'Children can be very sticky!' This one was. She hugged her close and walked into the light of the bonfire.

On his way back with more food to distribute, Julian

stopped dead as he caught sight of her, his face almost harsh as he stood looking at her with the child in her arms, and for a moment she was stunned at his expression. She tore her gaze away and walked on, more convinced than ever that she had to get away from him. For a moment she had imagined herself here with Julian's child, all this real, only love between them, a family of their own. But it would never be like that.

The fireworks display would have done justice to any gala, and Merissa was as enthralled as her small companion, watching the bursts of coloured lights, the blue and green and purple, the pinks and reds, bursting in patterns in the air. There was hardly a break between one breathtaking display and another, and the excited voices of the children showed their enjoyment.

Amongst it all, the one rocket that misfired could have been missed. It landed almost at the feet of one small boy, who was too scared to move. For a second everyone seemed dazed, then Merissa shook off the numbing fear for the child and leapt forward. She grasped it and using all her strength threw it out over the children and into the park, where it exploded in mid-air with a great shower of green stars.

It was beautiful now, not dangerous, but Merissa bit her lip hard to keep the cry of pain inside, slipping away quietly into the house. She hardly dared open her hand and look at the burn, she knew it was bad, and she searched rather wildly around the kitchen for something to stop the pain and cover her hand.

'Merissa!' She looked up guiltily as Julian strode in, his eyes on her drawn face. He had her hand in his before she could stop him, opening her fingers and seeing the ugly burn in a thick band across her palm.

'God—you're burned!' he muttered. 'I probably fixed that damned rocket!'

'More likely I did,' his father asserted, coming in too. 'You're a deal more efficient than I am, but right now, my lad, you're dithering. Come into my office, Merissa,' he went on, taking her firmly from Julian. 'I'll see to it for you. Splendid overarm bowling, that. Want to play in the local cricket team next season?'

Julian was simply left standing there alone, and Merissa was glad, because right now she would rather have rushed into his arms and cried like a baby than moved away from him. He had to be the one to draw away. He was staring at her with unreadable eyes and he made no move to follow. Maybe he was thinking she was as much a nuisance as he had said rather gently when she had had that allergic attack. She had, after all, spoiled the engagement party, and now here she was, burned and wilting, when there was a party here. She seemed to be jinxed as far as Julian was concerned.

She didn't know how she was going to get through Sunday, but Julian's father took care of that. He grabbed her straight after breakfast and took her to re-dress the burn, which was now well on the way to being better.

'Modern medicine,' he laughed at her surprise. 'A miracle of science and my quick actions. Now you can reward me by coming over to the church and letting me show you the ancient charms of this place.'

Julian appeared in the hall as they were leaving, and his father looked disappointed.

'I expect you'll want to come too?' he asked with humorous displeasure when he had announced their destination. 'I realise you've no desire to let her out of your sight, but I was hoping to have her to myself this morning.'

Merissa thought Julian would intervene, would think that she was about to confess all to his father, but he didn't seem to care any more.

'Be my guest!' he snapped. 'I expect she'll be as much at ease with you as she is with me.'

Edward Forrest grinned to himself and thereafter ignored the incident, and Merissa was at ease with him, intrigued by the old Saxon church, grateful that he shared her interest and was delighted by her knowledge.

'We're glad to see that Julian intends to settle down at last,' he confided as they stepped at last back out into the misty sunshine. 'He's thirty-six and it's time he had a wife and family. Alice and I are really happy about you, my dear.'

'Maybe I ought to tell you . . .' Merissa began, her nerve giving way when she thought of the great lie she was living, her mind also reeling from the fact that they did not resent her taking the place of Felicitiy. Julian had misjudged the situation there, but they treated Felicity like a daughter, and she couldn't understand the quiet and happy vibrations that ran through the house when to her it seemed Julian had involved them in so much of a tangle.

Her attempted confession was foiled, however, because Mr Forrest cut in as if he had never heard.

'Before I get you back to Julian, come and see the most wonderful Saxon cross. It's down in the churchyard by the wall. Should be restored, to my mind. Just look at this grass! A man is supposed to come and keep everything in order. I'll have to speak to the vicar about this. We only have services every other Sunday in this day and age, and he has two parishes to care for, but still, that's no excuse . . .'

He wandered around the old walls and Merissa followed, her courage waning. If she told him, he was going to be hurt too, and no doubt he would feel a fool. Damn you, Julian! You've made a complete muddle of my life and everybody else's, she thought bitterly.

Back at the house she went determinedly to search for him. She had had more than enough. How he was going to explain all this to his parents she did not know—that was his affair. She would have plenty of trouble explaining it to her own mother.

She could hear his voice in the garden and she was upon him before she realised that it was Felicity that he was speaking to. She could not see them because of a thick hedge, and neither could they see her, and as the content of the conversation dawned on her she blessed that fact, but she could not for the life of her make her steps either go away or go forward.

'Just how long to do you intend to keep this up, Julian?' Felicity was asking with none of the lonely and lost tone to her voice that she had been using to Julian before. 'I'm not going to keep it up for much longer. I like Merissa, and I won't continue to see her being hurt.'

'What in heaven's name makes you imagine she's hurt?' Julian rasped in exasperation. 'You promised to help, and I've still not got what I'm after.'

'You'll get what you're after by coming straight out with the truth!' Felicity remarked sharply. 'No wonder she's often on the defensive with you. As a woman I can see her point of view—you're a devil!'

'You've never had the need to be on the defensive with me,' muttered Julian. 'I treat you like a queen, always have done. That remark is totally unfair.'

'But we're not speaking about me, are we?' countered Felicity. 'You and I know where we stand. Merissa's being manipulated dreadfully, and she knows nothing about anything. If you don't get this settled soon I'll be on my way. I want that ring back on my finger, and nothing is going to keep it off for much longer! It shows my devotion to you that I was prepared to take it off in the first place. Your mother and father must be going blind! Every day I expect some comment. You really must get her out of here.'

'I'm taking her home right now,' Julian said quietly. 'Nothing is going as I originally planned. I'm in an utterly miserable fix!'

'So you should be, darling. I can't think why you didn't come straight out with the truth in the first place.'

'She'd have walked off later, still on the same path she was walking,' he retaliated. 'I want her in so deep that she can't get out.'

'And is that going to satisfy you?' Felicity asked softly.

'For want of anything more, yes!' he snapped. 'I'll find her and get her home.'

'You should stop calling Creswell House home for Merissa,' she said worriedly. 'She really shouldn't be there at all, and you know it.'

'She stays! I'm not letting her go—if she goes I might just as well have never bothered in the first place, and now—I just couldn't face losing.'

'She'll eventually decide that, when all's said and done,' Felicity said softly.

'Can't you say something nice and hopeful for a change?' Julian begged with a hard laugh, but clearly Felicity was no more amused than he was.

'I care about you, you idiot. The truth is always the best thing, after all.'

'Not yet,' he sighed. 'I've got too much to lose. I'll ring you next week.'

There was a sound of movement and Merissa fled, ashamed at listening in to the conversation and too muddled to try to analyse it. She would have to think it over later. Right now she had to beat Julian to the house. She just made it.

They left about an hour later with promises for an early return, and Merissa was both touched and grieved when Julian's mother and father both kissed her goodbye. She knew that as far as she was concerned, the promise would not be kept and she would never see them again. Julian seemed to be hurting a lot of people.

He was completely silent, and she took the opportunity to go over the conversation she had overheard in her mind, to see what she had learned. Obviously Felicity was not, as she had thought, heartbroken, and also there was a great deal of affection between her and Julian. It began to look as if nobody was being deceived except herself, and she even wondered if his mother and father were also in the picture, dismissing that almost as soon as the thought came. Felicity had said they must be blind not to have noticed the ring that was no longer on her finger. What ring? It could hardly be an announced engagement to Julian, or his mother and father would have demanded to know what was going on. Unless she and Julian were secretly engaged?

It somehow didn't add up. And what was it that Julian

was after? Her mind just skimmed back to the tapes, but she dismissed that as ridiculous at once. What couldn't he face losing? Puzzles of this magnitude with no clues were simply beyond her. She would just go. He had said he wanted her in so deeply that she wouldn't be able to get out later. In so deeply with what? Merissa closed her eyes against the brightness of the afternoon sun and gave up the battle with a deep sigh.

It drew Julian's attention.

'So you still intend to simply just go, Merissa?' he asked quietly in a voice she had never heard before.

'Yes!' She said it firmly and finally, to convince herself as well as him.

'When?' he shot out harshly. 'I want you to stay until tomorrow at least. If I thought you were going to walk into Creswell House and pack right there and then, I'd lock you up!'

'You couldn't,' she said wearily. 'Even you with your overpowering attitude couldn't do that.'

'I kidnapped you once,' he said softly. 'I could do it more easily now.'

'But you wouldn't.'

'No,' he agreed quietly, 'I wouldn't. If you don't want to be with me then there's not much point in forcing you to stay. Just stay until tomorrow, all right?'

'All right.' They both lapsed into gloomy silence until they arrived at the house.

'I have to go out for a while,' said Julian as he let her into the silence of the house. 'Be here when I get back, Merissa. You promised.' She nodded. It would be for the last time.

CHAPTER NINE

For a while Merissa simply wandered around the house, touching things she would never see again. She didn't even consider the idea of cooking for Julian tonight; the thought of sitting alone with him for the last time was far too painful. They would have to go out. She couldn't either bring herself to pack her things. It was all so final, so much the end of any dreams, and she sat staring out of the window as she thought of the very bleak future.

She was so puzzled too. Felicity was not the threat she was supposed to be, they were on the very best of terms, they cared about each other—and as for Louise, Julian could have dispatched her with a few well chosen words, he had plenty of those. No, it was, as Felicity had said, one complete lie, but why? What for?

If he had simply wanted her he could have pursued her in the time-honoured fashion; she knew she would have finally given in. Even at first sight of him her knees had turned to water and he knew it, so why the pretended engagement? Why this deep and devious lying? Merissa began to wonder what her role really was. The story of the other women had been merely a ploy to get her here to this house, and Julian's very real desire to keep her here was also tied in with his original reason. 'If she goes I might just as well have never bothered in the first place, and now—I just couldn't face losing.'

She thought over his words to Felicity, but nothing made any sense any more, and she was just about to force herself to pack when she heard the car in the drive and looking out of the window saw something that brought her heart right into her throat. Hugh Goddard's car, and Hugh stepping out of it.

If Julian came back, there would be murder! He hated Hugh! What madness had brought him here to this house? Merissa could only think of her mother and the fact that she had not phoned either all the weekend or since she had returned. She flew down the stairs and to the front door.

'Hugh! What is it?' She ran down the steps to meet him, frightened even more by the grim look of him. He advanced to meet her with tight lips and hard eyes.

'What are you and Forrest up to?' he demanded harshly. 'Right from the first I knew there had to be something very fishy going on, because a man like Forrest doesn't fall for a simpleton like you!'

Merissa stopped dead in her tracks, a mixture of feelings flooding over her. Her mother, then, was all right. This had nothing to do with her mother at all, this was some personal quest. She regretted now the fact that she was here in the open, the doorway so far behind her. Why, oh why did she do these impulsive things? Hugh looked dreadful, drawn and angry, his eyes a little wild, and she began to back stealthily to the door, trying not to be too obvious about it.

'What are you talking about? Do you realise how you've frightened me? When I saw you here, of all places, I thought something was wrong with Mother. I thought only something like that would have brought you here!' She decided to keep talking as she moved. He had a dangerous look about him, and she prayed hard that Julian would come, but she knew that was very unlikely. 'You surely know how Julian dislikes you! What possessed you to take the risk of coming here?'

'I know he's not here! I'm not really stupid, you know!' he snarled, slowly coming forward. 'I've had my eye on this house since I realised you were here. This is the first time I've had the chance to get you alone. I saw Forrest half an hour ago heading for town, and now I want a few truths from you. What are you up to? Why is Forrest almost haunting the place where he's put your mother?'

'He likes her! After all, we're getting married soon, and I'm too busy to go down to see Mummy daily, we take it in turn,' Merissa invented glibly. 'You know she's not always well! What's the matter with you, Hugh? You're behaving like a fool. For goodness' sake get out of here before Julian comes back. I've no idea why he dislikes you so much, but I know he does, and it's nothing to do with me. You and I have been friends for years. If there's something between you and Julian then it's none of my business, and certainly he hasn't taken me into his confidence. I just don't want him to come back and find you here. I don't want either of you to get hurt.'

Her attitude seemed to be convincing him, because some of the tension began to leave his shoulders and his face looked less wild. Even so, he still came forward, and Merissa gave the thing a last try out of sheer desperation.

'Look, Hugh, if this is bothering you so much then I'll really try to find out what he's up to, if you think there's something going on. Maybe I'll be able to get it out of him.'

The effect was astonishing. Hugh's face paled instantly and he was suddenly not threatening any more. Instead he was almost afraid.

'No!' he said loudly, then lowered his voice, forcing a smile. 'No, Merissa, thanks all the same, but maybe I'm getting a little neurotic. I suppose it's just plain jealousy. Forget it, love. Forget I came. I'm sorry.'

To her amazement, he simply turned and got back into his car, swinging it round and leaving with a cheery wave as she stepped back into the house and closed the door, making quite sure the Yale lock had caught. Neurotic? She was beginning to wonder if he wasn't after all quite raving mad. Her legs were still shaking as she made her way back up to her bedroom.

'The plot thickens!' she muttered to herself. What on earth was that all about? A mere matter of weeks ago she had been on the best of terms with Hugh. He was an old friend, someone who had worked for her father, a trusted helper, welcome at her home. Now he was, it seemed, suddenly unbalanced, raving about some sort of plot. He wasn't the only one who was feeling as if there was a plot either, and Merissa was not so stupid that she failed to see that there must be some connection.

She actually jumped as she heard a car, and this time she wasn't about to rush down the stairs and out into the dusk of the evening. She went to the window, peering carefully out, expecting to see Hugh back and returned to a menacing lunatic. There was menace right enough, but it was Julian!

He slammed out of the car and bounded up the steps, his

key already in his hand, and even from her window
Merissa could see trouble in large letters. It needed no great
intelligence to realise that he had passed Hugh on the way
in and drawn his own conclusions. She heard him coming
up the stairs and wished with all her might that there was
some way she could deny Hugh's visit. There wasn't,
though. Julian stormed into her room without knocking,
looking about twice his usual height with twice his normal
capacity for rage.

'So!' he grated. 'The moment I'm out, you entertain your
old lover! I must have been out of my mind not to think of it
before. The times you've had to get him here, the long
photographic session with Derrick Lean the other day! No
wonder you gave Mrs Patterson the time off so readily!
What do you do, phone him or wave a towel from your
bedroom window?'

'You're quite wrong,' said Merissa with a calm she
certainly did not feel. His eyes were brilliantly, coldly blue,
searing into her. He was white to the lips with rage, and she
stood her ground only by the help of a great deal of
courage. 'I'm not going to deny he was here, because I
assume you saw him leaving, but he was here only a matter
of minutes and he never came into the house.'

'He wouldn't need to this time, would he?' Julian rasped
savagely. 'All you had to do was tell him you were leaving
tomorrow! I expect he can wait one day to get his hands on
you!'

So enraged by this constant battering at her self-esteem,
so frustrated with bitterness and misery that she hardly
knew what she was doing, Merissa flew at him, storming
across the room with white-faced fury and launching
herself at him before he could react.

'You loathsome, arrogant, brutal pig!' she yelled, her fists
clenched and flying wildly, beating at him with frantic,
hammering blows. 'How dare you accuse me of anything at
all when you've done nothing but trick me and lie to
everyone I've ever seen you with, including your own
mother and father? You've forced me into things I never

thought I was capable of, and you dare to question my behaviour? I hate you! I hate you!'

Right at that moment she did, and it was very clear in her dark and angry eyes. Julian stopped her blows easily, grasping her wrists with cruel force and holding her in front of him, leaving her struggling uselessly, her hair all over her face and tears of wild rage falling down her flushed cheeks.

'Well, well!' he grated through clenched white teeth. 'This is very enlightening. What's this all about—sexual frustration? Did I come back too soon, before you could satisfy the cravings of that eager body? Don't fuss, sweetheart, a little thing like that can soon be taken care of.'

Fear replaced anger very quickly as he swept her up into his arms and dropped her still struggling on to the bed, coming down with her before she could roll away.

'Oh no, you don't!' he said grimly as her legs flew out to kick him and her hands clawed out at his face. It was so easy for him to force his greater strength on her, to trap her legs with one powerful leg and force her arms above her head.

'What now?' he asked derisively, looking into her blazing eyes. 'Do I satisfy you, or myself? There's a deal of difference between the two, and I really don't think there's any need to be gentle. We're right back where we started— right at the beginning, when I saw a girl who liked a good time and who later almost convinced me she was as soft and timid as a kitten. Now that I've seen the wildcat, my memory is all coming back. You want to forget the engagement OK, I agree! I'll just collect the debt you owe me and then you can go back to Goddard!'

He came down hard on top of her, forcing the breath from her, capturing her wildly tossing head by the simple expediency of clamping his lips on hers and forcing her mouth open. She couldn't move in any direction, and Julian was not going to release her. Her arms were aching above her head, her legs and body trapped, and his deep and violent kiss was making breathing almost impossible. She was stiff with panic, hot tears of fright and pain now welling up in her eyes and small murmurs of fear escaping from her constricted throat. This was another Julian, not the man she loved. She had lost that man, never even having owned him at all. There was only deceit, scorn and now fear. The tears spilled down and blended with their lips, and he suddenly relaxed, lifting his head and drawing her aching arms down to fold her against him, his own hand coming to move gently along her bruised lips, a bleak resignation in his face.

'Don't be frightened, Merissa,' he said softly, his breath leaving him in a deep and shaken sigh, his own face now looking strangely lost and lonely. 'I can't hurt you, surely you know that? I don't really believe Goddard has been here when I've been away either. I was just wildly jealous. I don't even want to know why he came.'

Merissa stared up at him, not attempting to free herself from the weight of his powerful body, wanting to touch his face and ease away that look of defeat that sat so squarely and unlikely on his face.

'He came to ask why . . .' she began quietly, her breath catching in a snatch of misery that had not left her, but Julian stopped her before she could continue, his fingers against her lips.

'No, don't tell me. I don't deserve to know, I don't want to know. He obviously didn't come to see me, and it's none of my business. Don't tell me, just stop being afraid of me, that's all. Whatever you did, I could never, never hurt you, even in anger. My anger with you just couldn't last that long.'

It was almost impossible to realise that they were still there on the bed, Julian's arms locking her to him, his body pressing her into the soft mattress. Moments before they had been locked in a frightening battle, a battle of physical subjugation, and now they were lying together, staring into each other's eyes, their breathing steadying and a realisation of the warmth of each other slowly sinking into them.

Merissa felt it in the slow shifting of his weight, in the

almost imperceptible movement of his body and the darkening of his blue eyes. Julian felt it too in her slow relaxation, in the hands that came softly to his chest and the way her limbs moved almost timidly to adjust to his.

His hand came to her face, tracing her cheeks, moving along her lips, smoothing her hair back behind her ears, and there was a depth of longing in his glance as he searched her flushed face, his lips slightly smiling with a rueful acceptance of the situation.

'If I kiss you,' he murmured softly, 'will you fight me? Will you think I'm attacking you?'

'No.' Merissa shook her head, blinking away the tears, and he smoothed them from her cheeks and eyes with unsteady fingers, kissing each eye closed, kissing her hot cheeks but making no attempt to claim her mouth.

'Will that do?' he asked gently. 'Do you want me to go?'

She shook her head, her eyes clinging to his and then moving to the firm and sensuous lips so close to her own, seeing them smile and come closer until she closed her eyes and waited for his mouth to cover her own.

It was gentle and deep, asking nothing but making her want to give everything. Her own lips parted and he accepted her gift, his mouth searching hers deeply, moving with a growing hunger against hers, his body hardening at her soft and sweetly offered submission.

'I want you,' he whispered, lifting away a little but still brushing her lips with his. 'I want you, but you're going to have to tell me it's what you want too. You're going to have to show me that I'm not forcing my desire on you. I want everything, but only if you want to give it to me.'

Merissa opened her eyes to find his eyes so close, darkened and filled with a growing desire that he held tightly on leash, and her hands lifted to do what they had wanted so often to do, to stroke his face, to curl in the crispness of his hair, to trace the long dark brows and touch the thickly curling lashes, the tight, strong line of his jaw.

'The words, Merissa!' he breathed against her lips. 'I need to know!'

She moved against him, thrilled by the hard power of his body, a sigh of deep contentment leaving her throat as she felt his immediate response and her arms wound softly around his neck.

'Julian!' she begged shakily. 'Love me!'

Suddenly his waiting body came to life, his possessive hand lifting her breast, his arm tightening her to him.

'I will, Merissa!' he groaned, his mouth opening above hers hungry and demanding. Her words had opened the floodgates of desire and she knew he could not, would not stop, and she didn't want him to stop. She had come to a decision, made up her mind. The engagement would stay, she would marry him if he still wanted that. As to the future, it would have to take care of itself. For now there was only Julian and their great need for each other, and everything within her welcomed him as he clasped her to him with a desperate energy.

'Darling! Darling!' He tore off the fine high-necked sweater he had been wearing, pulling it impatiently over his head and tossing it aside, his hands urgently on the buttons of her blouse. 'I want to be close to you. I want to touch you so much that it hurts.' He lifted her, sitting beside her and holding her against him as he slid the blouse away and unclipped her lacy bra, his hands warm and gentle on her smooth back. 'My lovely Merissa!' he said thickly, easing her back to the bed and pulling her against his hard chest. 'I seem to have been waiting for you for a lifetime at least, maybe longer. The first moment I saw you, I knew. Since then every moment has been spent in waiting for you, waiting to feel you close to me, wanting me.'

The same frenzy to be part of him was in Merissa too, and when they were finally clasped tightly together, their clothes discarded, her breath left her in a great sigh of contentment as her arms clung to his shoulders and her lips planted small heated kisses on the warm skin of his face.

'Merissa! Sweetheart, I can't wait for you!' he gasped desperately when her twisting and arching body had driven him to the very edge of madness. 'You're like a wild flame. You make me wild too! I want you now, darling!'

She was only just able to hear him, his searching hands and lips had robbed her of all power of thought and only the painful aching inside was a reality. He lifted her to him, parting her thighs, claiming her body with a force that brought a sharp cry of pain from her lips, and Julian stiffened in equal shock, perfectly still above her, his eyes wide and brilliantly blue, his face stunned. 'Merissa!' His husky cry sounded like an accusation, a denial of both their needs, and she held tightly to him, her lips searching anxiously for his.

'Don't leave me! Don't leave me, Julian! Please!'

'I can't!' he groaned. 'Oh, Merissa, you wild and wonderful little idiot!' The driving force turned into tenderness, his arms crushingly possessive and strangely protective, her name on his lips as he took them together into a light and dreamless place where they were alone, wildly spinning above the earth.

When reality returned, she expected a reckoning, recriminations, almost anything from annoyance to being ignored, but his arms never left her for one minute and his lips eased their deep searching to brush gently along her trembling mouth as his hands smoothed her hair and stroked her shaking body.

'So now,' he said gently, 'I understand a whole lot more. If I'd understood earlier, I wouldn't have hurt you.'

'You wouldn't have wanted me either,' she murmured. She was still dazed and filled with a stunned kind of happiness, not really thinking about what she said at all, and his quiet laughter made her open her eyes and look at him.

'How is it that such a very clever man as John Troy managed to get himself such an idiotic daughter?' Julian asked softly. 'Being a virgin isn't a punishable crime, my sweet. It's only a crime to stay that way when we need each other so much. If I'd known, though, I would have understood so much more about you.'

He tilted her face to his with one arrogant hand and his

eyes blazed down into hers. 'Going to marry me, then?' he asked fiercely. 'Don't think you're going to get away now. That ring stays exactly where it is. Any battling we do can be done on a family basis.'

'I've finished battling,' Merissa said quietly, her eyes moving over his dearly loved face with a kind of yearning that darkened his eyes again.

'Let me look at that burn,' he said gruffly, taking her hand and gently opening her fingers. 'Do you know how I felt when that happened? I wanted to comfort you, to love it all better, and you wouldn't let me. I had absolutely no rights. I even felt I had no right to follow you when my father carted you off to see to it. Marry me!' he added fiercely and harshly. 'You're mine!'

'I've not got much choice, have I?' Merissa asked winsomely, and Julian's face darkened quickly as he stared into her eyes.

'Why?' he asked threateningly, obviously thinking propriety was forcing this admission on to her.

'Because I want to, and if you want to as well, then what else is there to do?' She smiled into his darkened eyes, and he bent his head to kiss her hard and fast.

'Little nuisance!' he muttered. His eyes came back to her hand. 'It's almost better. Think what you'll be getting out of the bargain, sweetheart—a free doctor who can work small miracles!'

'He's really good,' Merissa mused, her own eyes on the fast healing burn. 'It *is* almost better.'

'Are you better, Merissa?' he murmured softly, his lips caressing the remaining traces of her burn. She couldn't answer really because she knew what she had invited with her love and her decision to marry him. He would love her fiercely for as long as it lasted, and then there would be unhappiness for them both. She had belonged to him in her heart for some time, maybe even since that first sight of him, and there was no possibility of recovery. Her eyes showed her distress as they sought to avoid his.

'Regrets?' he asked with a tender kiss on her still hot

cheek, and she lifted her head, her dark eyes searching his face for some sign of love, anything to give her hope. She saw only desire, that and an odd tenderness she could not quite understand.

With a little cry, she moved against him, pressing her lips to his, and he gathered her against the growing arousal of his body, his voice warm and deeply triumphant.

'I think this is going to be the second time right now,' he said thickly. 'I don't think I'm ever going to be able to resist you.'

He pulled her against him swiftly and determinedly, his hands not so gentle now. Before he had realised her innocence, tempering his needs to match her inexperience, but now she felt the full force of his desire, the driving intensity of a man who wanted to possess her with an almost savage longing, and she reacted automatically, moving with him, her kisses almost as hot as his own until he cried out her name in an agonised voice and lifted her to meet the hard thrust of his body.

'That was inevitable,' he said later as he held her still trembling in his arms. 'That's how I've wanted you, needed you—and don't ever look at me again as you did then, with that sad, unsure little glance, with those strange, lovely eyes filling with tears, because that's what will happen every time you do it. Nothing is going to take you away from me. You're home, Merissa. I've got you, and you're mine!'

She never answered. Already she was drifting into sleep, almost faint with happiness, thinking of nothing but the here and now. Dimly she heard Julian's voice, heard him say her name, but she was beyond any replies, her only answer a smile of contentment which he saw because she heard his soft laughter and felt his possessively stroking hands on her as she fell into a deep sleep. She knew she was home. She had always known since the first moment he had touched her.

Incredibly, Merissa slept all night, and she knew when she awoke that only hunger had awakened her now. The only sign that the night before had not been some erotic dream was the imprint of Julian's head on the pillow beside her, because he was not there.

She hesitated to go and find him, wondering if, with the coming of the day and the assuaging of his desire, he was filled with regret, wondering if he would face her with anger, even though the anger would be directed at himself, but the need to eat drove her to the shower and to dress, and when she got downstairs, he was not there.

There was a note for her, propped up on the toaster, and she opened it with trembling fingers.

'Had to go out,' it said briefly. 'Don't move until I get back.' There was nothing else, it wasn't even signed, and she was still filled with uncertainty, still moving between the wonder of a night in Julian's arms and the memory of his previous scorn and anger. She didn't know what to do, except that she couldn't ever go now. She doubted if she had ever really been capable of simply walking away from Julian.

After breakfast she remembered that there was a small backlog of work, Mrs Patterson still being away, and she began to determinedly clean and polish around the house, keeping her body occupied and her mind blank until she realised it was almost lunchtime. She was on her way to the kitchen when the telephone rang, and it was Clare.

'I'm glad I found you in, Merissa,' she said, not sounding surprised that Merissa should be there. 'The jobs are rolling in thick and fast, just as I expected they would. I could do with you coming round to work out some kind of schedule. I think we could accept quite a lot of them.'

'I—er—tomorrow. I'll come tomorrow,' Merissa said vaguely. A few days ago she would have been delighted, but now it meant nothing. She wanted to be with Julian, and nothing more, but she was still uneasy, uncertain.

'By the way, I hope I'll be invited to the wedding,' Clare went on. 'I can't say I wasn't a bit miffed at being left out of the engagement party.'

'It—it happened so quickly, and Julian . . .'

'I know. I spoke to your mother, that's how I knew where you were. He's certainly taken you out of circulation rapidly, but no excuses about the wedding invitation, my girl. I might have known he'd go after you after his reaction to you at the Fitzpatrick's opening. Maybe it was the way you just ran out and left him standing there. When I told him who you were he just stood there staring after you as if you were something he'd always been looking for and after that, nothing could put him off. I felt really guilty about joining in the deception to get you to do the photographs for the new centre, but I knew it would pay off, and it has. Mind you, I never thought he'd be sweeping you off your feet—oddly enough, his interest didn't seem to be like that at all. I must be getting old!'

Merissa didn't hear much of the rest of the call. It was dawning on her that after Julian's initial and hunting looks when he had seen her with Hugh, his real interest had grown since he knew who she was. Certainly, that day in the car, he had told her that he knew, but by then he had almost everything he wanted. His real pursuit of her had been from the moment he knew that she was John Troy's daughter.

The women in his life were no threat at all. Of the many women he had given her to understand were such a threat to him, only two had materialised, Louise and Felicity. There was no doubt that he and Felicity were on the very best of terms, had known each other for a very long time, and that Felicity was in possession of information that Julian was keeping from everyone else, including his parents. Louise was nothing at all, nothing that he could not have dealt with in about ten minutes. He and Felicity were as close as a brother and sister or very old friends.

It was confirmed by her next call. Julian's mother rang almost as soon as Clare had finished speaking, and her call answered a lot of unsolved problems.

'Oh, Merissa dear, you're there?' She obviously had no idea that Merissa was staying at Creswell House, and Merissa thought it was a good thing she didn't; her reaction would have been no more enthusiastic than her own mother's had been. 'Is Julian there, dear?'

'No, he—he's popped out for a minute.' Merissa found her face reddening even though she was alone. It seemed to her guilty mind that the whole world must know where she had spent the night, but Mrs Forrest went on quite happily.

'Well, give him a message and I'll ring later. Tell him Donald will be home in two weeks and that the wedding can go ahead as planned.'

'Donald?' Once again she was in the dark, trying to pretend she knew things that she had no idea about, and Julian's mother tutted at the other end of the line.

'Honestly—I really wonder what's got into that boy! He told you nothing of the children's party when he knew perfectly well you'd be a part of it, and now it seems he hasn't even mentioned his own brother! I suppose it would have come up more naturally if Felicity hadn't spent so much time feeling under the weather and keeping to her room—still, that's no excuse for Julian. I'll tell you myself. Donald is Julian's older brother. He's an engineer and he's been in India for about four months, his firm is building a huge bridge out there, but he'll be back in two weeks and the wedding can go ahead. He and Felicity can keep their plans intact and marry during his leave. She'll go back there with him afterwards. I feel really silly telling you this when you're almost part of the family yourself. I'll certainly speak to Julian! It must be love, I've never known him be absent-minded and inefficient before in his whole life.'

So now Merissa knew who had given Felicity the ring, a ring she had unwillingly taken from her finger to help Julian. She sat down, stunned and puzzled, as Mrs Forrest said goodbye. She had now worked it all out, except for one thing—why? It was easy to see that the invention of a great dilemma with these women had been an assistance in getting her to come here to live at the house, but why had he wanted that in the first place? He was quite capable of great persuasion as far as she was concerned. He could have slowly pursued her, been wherever she was, charmed her. She knew that finally it would have had the same results if desire had been his only motive—but it wasn't, she was sure of that.

There was her mother, there was Hugh and there were the tapes and the cottage. Merissa took a deep breath and rang her mother; she had to find out more, and if her mother knew anything, then she was going to have to get it out of her. There was no need. Her mother was, as usual, full of the idea of Julian.

'Julian? Why, he was here almost as soon as it was light. I wasn't even up!' Now she knew where Julian had gone. He had shrugged off the night before as if it had never been. It had changed her whole life, and yet it meant nothing to him. He had simply gone out and completed his plans. Got what he wanted.

'He's on his way back now, Merissa,' her mother continued. 'I know now what he was looking for. If he'd told me before I could have saved him a whole lot of trouble. When I went down he was sitting sunk into gloom and he asked me if there was any last tape that your father had brought in. Well, of course I could tell him, because I've never seen your father so angry as he was that day. I followed him into the study and I saw exactly where he put the tape. The position hadn't been altered in the removal and I was able to put my hand straight on it. You should have seen Julian's face. He played a few seconds of it and then he walked out into the kitchen and picked me straight up in the air! He was simply bursting with joy! He gave me one great hug and then went tearing off. I've no idea what it was,' she added in answer to Merissa's question. 'Not music, though, just talk.'

Just talk—yes, now Merissa knew! Her father's experiment and, no doubt, the results. Anger boiled up and mixed with grief in her mind. The puzzle was complete. Julian had what he was after, and his words swam in her mind as she remembered his conversation in the hall with Dick Finley. 'I only need the tape and then we're home and dry.'

They were planning to make use of her father's work, and she had been the means of gaining access to it, the road that led to her mother. Last night had meant nothing to him at all. She felt sick and numb.

CHAPTER TEN

THERE was no mistaking the sound of triumph in Julian's voice when he finally came in. Merissa heard his car and his keys in the door and then he was in the hall, calling to her as soon as he was inside.

'Merissa! I'm here!' Just as if everything was real, as if she meant as much to him as he did to her. She stayed where she was, unable to face him, not even answering, but he did not come to find her. He was too filled with the glee of having got what he had been searching for. 'I'll be in the study!' As he called again, she forced herself into action. He had tricked her, made a fool of her, hurt her so completely that her anger surfaced and pulled her out of her misery. She walked down the stairs and into the study, her face pale but determined.

He was already on the phone, and she heard his final words as she walked in.

'I'll contact you later in the day, but we have everything now. Bring the rest of the documentation when you leave the firm—and Dick, you can move out for good now. In future, you're working with me.'

He looked round as Merissa came in, the triumph and pleasure dying from his face at the expression on hers, and she waited until the call was finished and then gave him no chance to speak.

'Don't bother to tell me!' she snapped bitterly. 'I already know everything! You've got everything you wanted, you've got my father's tape, and now the bargain is over, the job finished! But if you imagine I'm simply going to walk off and let you use my father's knowledge and hard work, then you can think again! The tape isn't yours and I want it. Before I leave, I get that tape!'

She turned to walk away. The effort to look into Julian's face and accuse him had been so great that she had to get out of the room. She had no protection against the cool and surprised blue eyes.

'What do you imagine is on this tape, Merissa?' His voice, surprisingly quiet and oddly enough threaded with the sound of pain, stopped her, and she swung back to look at him.

'I know what's on the tape—there's no imagination required! You've got what you were after, what all this has been about—my father's work on the new process!' He made no attempt to answer, no denial, nothing, and she raved on, hurting badly so that her voice was hard and brittle. 'There was no trouble with women, was there? I can't imagine any situation with women or with anything else, for that matter, that you couldn't handle yourself, especially with the help of Felicity, your future sister-in-law!' He made no comment about her newly acquired knowledge, in fact the only sign that he had even registered her comment was a dark, raised eyebrow.

'Your mother was on the phone,' Merissa continued bitterly. 'Donald will be home soon, well in time for the wedding! You only wanted me to be here to have a constant excuse to get to my mother and the tape. Well, now you've done it, you've succeeded! What's the next move? An offer in a share of the proceeds if we keep quiet? There's no way I can be silenced!'

She turned away again and walked towards the door, but she never even reached it. His own anger mounting by the second, Julian pounced on her and spun her round, glaring into her eyes.

'There is a way you can be silenced, and we both know it!' he rasped angrily. 'However, we'll get to that later. First you'll hear the tape—you'll hear it if I have to tie you in a chair!'

There was no gentleness in the way he handled her as he marched her across to the desk, pushing her into a chair before she could protest, slamming the tape into a cassette recorder and towering over her with threatening, icy eyes as he switched on the machine.

'Now you'll listen! This is the last time you'll turn that vicious little tongue on me!'

Merissa heard the tape begin, steeling herself to hear the sound of the well remembered voice, but her hurt and her temper drained away as she realised that it was not her father's voice at all, it was a voice she had never heard before.

At first there was only puzzlement on her face, then her anger and her colour drained away as she began to get the drift of the message. It was a tape from an answering machine, and the subject of the call was her father.

'He'll find himself out of that laboratory within two weeks, with neither equipment nor credit-worthiness. With two hundred thousand in debts to pay off, he'll be ripe for an offer to rejoin us on any terms. The banks are just about ready to move in—we've established that.'

Merissa hardly heard the rest, as she had hardly heard the beginning. Her eyes met Julian's and he looked at her coldly. He was now the man she had first met, scornful, arrogant and way above her. There was no trace of the tenderness he had shown last night, no sign of desire and not one flicker of sympathy in his cold blue eyes. He was hard and unforgiving, his anger seeming to be directed both at her and the voice on the tape.

'Heard enough?' He flicked the machine off and stood stiffly in front of her as she sat stunned and silent in the chair. 'I detected no secret plans on the tape, no formulas. You've just been listening to a conspiracy, a conspiracy to ruin a man and take away his good name, his whole future. If you imagine you were used so that I could get this evidence, then I can only tell you you're right. I considered your feelings were secondary to this. In the matter of John

Troy's name and reputation, I felt you were completely expendable!'

'Who was the tape intended for?' Merissa refused to let the hard voice penetrate her mind, refused to understand the words that were aimed at her so cruelly.

'The tape was for Hugh Goddard!' he grated. 'Only fate let it fall into your father's hands. Unfortunately, fate also allowed him to be killed in a car accident on the same day.'

Tears sprang into her eyes, but he ignored them, turning away and beginning to pace restlessly about as he spoke, his hands deep in his pockets, his tall frame taut with anger.

'When your father left Ponton's,' he told her, 'Hugh Goddard left too and joined him almost at once. He too, apparently, was not pleased with events at the firm, and as he'd been an accountant with them, he took over the business side of your father's affairs. I imagine John was quite happy to leave things to him—your father was always more interested in the practical side of things than in any money-making concerns.

'Ponton's lost business at an alarming rate. People wondered why your father had moved, and without his name, there were many firms who moved their business elsewhere. Your father began to do very well indeed. I don't think you realise just how honoured his name was in the industry. His ideas were years ahead of other people's. His integrity was unquestioned and his advice as a consultant drew big firms in his direction. And Ponton's wanted him back. They had to get him back!

'Goddard never ceased to be on the payroll of Ponton's; he was with your father merely as a spy and to work him into trouble. He was very successful, because your father was not in any way a business man, he never ceased to be an idealist and an intellectual. Bills were not paid, thousands were squandered, and there were two sets of books, one for your father to see, and the real ones. Goddard did very well indeed out of it for himself, his life-style is way above his income.'

He stopped pacing and looked down at her with a weary

sigh as he saw the tears streaming down her face, but he made no move to comfort her and there was no softening of his expression.

'How—how do you know all this? How can you prove it?' Merissa asked tremulously, wiping the tears with the back of her hand, refusing to face him, her eyes downcast.

'Dick Finley,' said Julian quietly. 'The man who interrupted us so fortunately a little time ago. He was also one of your father's old students, and they met again when your father went to Ponton's. It was from Dick that your father learned how they were cutting corners on the building, and later, Dick found out that there was some kind of conspiracy going on to get at your father. He never found out what, but on the day that one of the directors so foolishly left this message on Goddard's answering machine, Goddard wasn't at work, he had 'flu. Your father was trying to do two jobs at once, Goddard's and his own, and I can imagine his rage when he heard this. Before he left the office to go home, he phoned Dick, told him about the tape and about the other set of books that he suspected were in Goddard's possession. He took the tape home for security, but he never told Dick that.

'On the way out that evening to meet Dick and to plan what to do, he was killed. Dick then waited for it all to come out as the firm went into liquidation, but it didn't. There was no tape, no books. The debts stood and Ponton's rolled on smugly as ever—until now!' he finished with a menacing certainty. 'Dick's been snooping for about two years and he contacted me as soon as I was back in England. He knew I'd want to do something about it, but by then, John Troy's widow and daughter seemed to have disappeared off the face of the map.'

He glared down at Merissa as if she had done everything deliberately.

'I traced Goddard and I began to haunt him. I wanted to make him uneasy, and I succeeded. We had one very unpleasant meeting right at the beginning and I let him know that there was evidence and I was just waiting to get the rest. It had one good effect, he dared not openly return to Ponton's, and he was living on a knife edge. Then I saw him with you!' He turned away from her and she felt his disgust. How could she have known all this? How could she know that Hugh Goddard was the man at the bottom of all their miseries?

'Anyway, we have all we need now and he'll have to turn out the books. Now they pay! John Troy's name will be cleared and Ponton's will face everything. They'll also pay off the two hundred thousand, if they survive. One or two of them will face imprisonment—especially Goddard!' Julian finished with savage satisfaction.

'It's not two hundred thousand now,' Merissa whispered, her head bent. 'It's a hundred and eighty thousand. I—I can't remember the exact number of pence.' She stood and wiped her eyes as he stared at her.

'What are you talking about?' he asked, not moving an inch.

'I—we—my mother and I have been paying it off. I could only manage five thousand a year. We had to live too, even if it was only in that awful little house, and we . . .'

She broke off as he strode forward, grasping her shoulders and breathing her name in an unbelieving voice.

'Merissa! What are you saying? You've been paying those astonishing debts? How long did you intend to go on, for the rest of your life?'

'My mother wanted it that way,' she said quietly, breaking away from him and moving across the room. 'I wanted it too. We knew it couldn't be true. When—when he died they said he'd made thousands. They wanted to know where it was. We felt like criminals. They—they took everything, the house, the car, most of the furniture . . .' Her voice broke and she walked resolutely further away, taking a deep shuddering breath. 'If you'd explained at first, if you'd told me all this . . .'

Her voice trailed away into misery. Julian would never know how much his silence had cost her, he would never know how much she loved him. Perhaps if he had told her and they had worked together to clear her father's name she would never have fallen in love with him. But even as she thought it, she knew it wasn't true. She would have loved him anyway, and he had only been using her, he had never ceased to be disgusted with her, and she had been— and still was—expendable.

She heard him move restlessly and sigh.

'Maybe if I'd never seen you with Goddard in the first place I would have acted differently. I saw you and wanted you myself, and it was such a good way of killing two birds with one stone. I knew that his women came and went fast, but you looked different, he seemed to be more than usually interested, and you were so young. I wanted to take everything he had away, and I certainly wanted to take you away. I wanted you on sight.' He moved closer, his words cutting like a knife.

'By the time I had you in my grasp, so to speak, I was convinced you were definitely not your father's daughter, not as you should be. There was Goddard and your way of life, your mother there, while you seemed to think of nothing but money—I didn't realise why until now! I wanted to get you where I could have some influence on you. I could see the road you were treading, or at least, I imagined I could.' He laughed softly, a laugh utterly without humour. 'I was determined to mould you into the sort of girl that John would have been proud of, but that was secondary. Mainly I wanted to see your mother and search for the tapes. Felicity reluctantly agreed to help me. Unfortunately, my plans blew up in my face.'

'Because I'm not at all someone you can alter,' Merissa finished for him, keeping her voice steady with great difficulty.

'Because I kissed you,' he corrected quietly, 'and in my arms you changed into another person. You were so vulnerable, so sweet, looking at me with big dark eyes. The puzzle started the night we announced our engagement to your mother, and I was so captivated that I nearly came straight out with the whole story then.'

'Why didn't you?' She turned on him with dark, accusing eyes. 'Why did you have to carry on the deception?'

'I wanted you,' Julian confessed softly, 'and it was nothing to do with Goddard. That first time I kissed you, everything seemed to explode. My conscience was swamped by the way I felt about you, and since then it's been damned hard. I seem to have spent more time trying to get close to you than getting close to the tapes. I've been trying to get under your act—and it is an act, isn't it, Merissa? The only protection you've had against the world since your father died and left you with a sick mother and enough debts to last you for the rest of your life.'

Merissa turned away abruptly, her heart beating anxiously. Julian couldn't really know that. If he realised then he would realise that she loved him, and there was then nothing but to stay here until he was tired of her.

'Now that you've solved everything,' she said as coldly as she could manage, 'you realise I haven't the slightest intention of marrying you or keeping this engagement up. You have the tape and I have all the debts off my back. I'll explain to Mother, and pretty soon I'll be able to get her a very nice cottage of her own. Clare says business is booming as far as I'm concerned.'

'You're not going anywhere!' rasped Julian, then he seemed to get a hold on himself. 'I want you to stay,' he added more quietly. 'I've never wanted you to go, and you know that. Your father's affairs are not now the biggest thing in my life, Merissa. You are that. I need you.'

'Until we're good friends and old companions?' she asked scathingly.

'I deserved that,' he confessed wryly. 'Desperation makes one say and do the most ridiculous things. I thought you didn't want to be anywhere permanently—except perhaps with your mother. I didn't dare to tell you the truth.'

'Even when Felicity told you you should?' she asked, turning dark and bitter eyes on him.

'So you heard that conversation?' he asked, his eyes blue

and intent on her face.

'Why not? Eavesdropping is quite within my character!'

'Not really.' He watched her closely, his eyes searching her face for some sign that she could not fathom. 'You've got enormous courage,' he told her softly, 'but I'm not going to let you walk away from me, not without a fight.'

'There's nothing to fight about,' she said, willing him to stop looking at her like that. 'We can now discuss the plans to use the information you've collected and then I'll go.'

'I don't think you've been listening,' he said dangerously. 'I haven't been talking about your father for some time, I've been talking about you, about us. There's no way you're going to walk out of my life.'

'There's no way you can prevent me.' Merissa turned away, but his voice was sharp and decisive.

'There is! I can never let you out of my arms. The moment I touch you, you give in. But I don't want that. I want you here legally and permanently. I want you married to me before Felicity and Donald are married. I've already told my father that, and it can be arranged.'

'You've told your father? How dare you?'

'How dare I not? I can't manage without you and I'm quite prepared to admit it. What about you admitting the same thing, Merissa?'

'There's no need to go to such lengths just because you want me!' She turned and stared at him rather wildly, unable to believe her ears, and he smiled for the first time, a slow smile of self-deprecation, shaking his head ruefully.

'Because I love you,' he said with a shrug, and she turned away, her body tight.

'We've put all our cards on the table now,' she reminded him quietly. 'Don't keep pretending. Just come out with the truth and see how it sounds!'

'All right,' Julian agreed quietly. 'I saw you with Goddard and I wanted you. Not a very commendable reason for going after you, I expect you'll think, but it was a feeling so strong and overwhelming that it was really something special. Then came the day when we met him in the street and he put his arms around you. There was nearly murder in the streets! I suddenly realised I loved you, that this was no longer a passionate pursuit, no longer a trick to get what I wanted. No matter who else had ever held you, no one else was ever going to, and I knew that if you walked out of my life I would never feel for anyone else what I feel for you. I know what your opinion is of me, Merissa,' he added quietly when she still turned away and kept silent, 'but I want to marry you, to love you and care for you for the rest of my life. You want me, and for now that will have to do. Maybe later, when all this deceit is forgotten, you'll be able to trust me and care for me a little. I know how much you've been hurt and I know how much I've hurt you, but I'll never hurt you again. I only want to see you happy.'

She couldn't believe the happiness that was welling up inside. For so long, everything had gone wrong in her life, and she felt this must be a dream, a dream she dared not believe in. She stood quite still, not daring to turn and show her face, and Julian moved then. He was behind her before she knew it, his movements swift and silent.

'Are you going to speak to me?' he asked deeply. 'Are you going to put me out of my misery one way or the other?'

When she still made no move, he took her shoulders gently and turned her to face him.

'You're crying! Am I as bad as all that, darling?' he asked wryly, his face under control, although there was a tremor in his voice that told her his emotions were under a tight rein.

'You're terrible!' she wept, tears streaming down her face. 'You've tricked me and lied to me, bullied me and hurt me, and I'd like to punish you really hard, but I love you too much!' She flung her arms around his neck and he pulled her into his arms almost roughly, his breath a deep sigh of relief as he folded her against him, rocking her in his arms, his hand stroking her hair. For a moment there was silence, only Merissa's little sounds of growing happiness punctuating the quiet of the room.

'Could you possibly manage to tell me that again?' Julian

asked softly as he lifted her face in a while to kiss away the last tears. 'Just three little words so that I don't begin to imagine I've dreamed it all.'

'I love you,' she said, looking up at him, an endearing enchantment on her face, and there was no time to say more, because his lips closed over hers, kissing her with such passion and tenderness that everything else left her mind and she nestled in his arms, her own arms tightly round him.

'I think we'd better stop right there,' he said after a while when she was breathless and totally lost in the magic of just being in his arms, even more so now that she knew it was real and for ever. 'We have a lot to talk about, and this is going to get us to one place only. Come over here and sit down. I could do with sitting down myself—I think my legs are shaking!'

He led her to the biggest chair and pulled her into it with him. 'As close as I can get you under the circumstances,' he said determinedly, pulling her against him. 'I'm not sure how long it will be before I can feel safe when you're out of my arms, but for now I'm not taking any chances. I can't let you go for even one second.'

Merissa didn't want to go anywhere. She curled up as close as he wanted her to be, looking up into his face, feeling that she had to keep her eyes on him for ever to bathe in the happiness that the clear blue gaze promised, eyes that had sometimes been hard and scornful but which now were soft and gentle.

'Oh, I've been fooling myself right from the beginning,' he sighed, watching her changing expressions with deep tenderness. 'Right from the word go, I caught glimpses of the sweet girl you are. Even on that platform there was hurt in your eyes, but you convinced me so often that I was mistaken, and I was so sure you belonged to Goddard.'

'Why did you bring Felicity into the plans?' Merissa asked softly. 'It was a big risk. At any time the truth might have come out quite naturally.'

'When I hit on my master plan to get you where I could keep an eye on you,' Julian confessed, 'I was a bit short of names to make it seem real. I don't really have a pack of females in tow. Felicity's name just popped into my head and I said it. I asked her permission later and she was furious! When Donald finds out, he'll want to break my bones,' he added with a grin. 'Anyway, she reluctantly agreed, but she wouldn't have gone on any longer, she likes you too much.'

'What about Louise?' asked Merissa with a frown, and he laughed into her eyes.

'No way!' he said firmly. 'She tried really hard, but I told you, my love, she's never been here except as a guest with other guests.' He kissed her nose. 'I've never invited her up those stairs, or any other stairs, for that matter.'

'She was very convincing!' Merissa persisted with a frown, and he tilted her face to his.

'I've never made love to her,' he said firmly, watching her face with intent eyes, threading his fingers through her shining hair. 'Do you want to stop feeling uneasy now and start feeling safe with me?'

It was impossible to remember anything when he kissed her, and when later she lay dreamily in his arms she really had to think hard to ask the few questions that still puzzled her.

'Why did you get me in with Derrick Lean? It wasn't necessary.'

'I wanted to give your career a boost,' he explained. 'I didn't want ever to see you again at a place like that nightclub where everyone was staring at you and people like me were asking for dates. I wanted to lift you right out of that sort of thing, it wasn't suitable for John Troy's daughter. Of course,' he added ruefully, 'later I didn't want half of London staring at your picture either. I wanted to be the only one to see you. I seem to have made a mess of things.'

'No, you haven't,' she said urgently. 'Right from the beginning you made me think about where my life was leading. You made me realise that I could easily become the hard person I was pretending to be if I wasn't careful. I was just hurt, though, when you kept saying you wanted me and didn't want to tie me down.'

'Darling,' he whispered against her hair, 'I've always wanted to tie you down! I never wanted to let you out of my sight, but I thought you'd leave me if I offered to make things permanent.'

'You always seemed to be threatening me,' complained Merissa with a little laugh. 'What was Plan B anyway? I remember being threatened with the last alternative.'

'Ah, that!' murmured Julian looking thoroughly pleased with himself. 'Well, finally I had to put Plan B into effect. You were determined to leave me and there was no other solution.'

'I don't remember!' She sat up straight and stared at him with wide dark eyes.

'Don't you?' he asked seductively. 'I'll remember last night for ever.'

'You brute!' she exclaimed, blushing so deeply that she had to hide her face.

'If I was a brute,' he laughed quietly, 'it was you who drove me to the end of my tether, with those clinging arms. You're the most cuddlesome person I've ever known.'

'I'd better be!' she threatened, winding her arms around his neck. 'Anyway,' she teased, 'I could still have walked out of your life.'

'Merissa, don't?' he pleaded in an agonised voice, suddenly very serious and still, and she fell silent too, her body melting against him.

'I love you, Julian,' she murmured as his lips closed over hers with determined possession. 'I've never loved anyone else and I never will. Every time you look round, I'll be there.'

'No more teasing!' Julian ordered later when he was prepared to allow her to breathe. 'I can't take it, not for years. I'm dreading even letting you go out to the shops, but if you want to,' he added with a quick grin, 'I expect I'll be proud of you doing your modelling. Maybe I'll go round London and pester passers-by, telling them that the girl on the posters is mine.'

'I used to think,' Merissa confessed softly, 'that if a

miracle happened, I'd want to go back to university, but now I find I'm utterly content with the miracle itself. I'll keep my hand in with the modelling for a while, though, I think.'

'When we come back from honeymoon,' he said firmly. 'We'll be in Canada for a good while.'

'Canada!' Merissa shot upright to stare into his smiling face. 'Surely you're not taking me to Niagara Falls for my honeymoon! I thought you could come up with something different—a Julian Forrest original.'

'Well,' he confessed, 'I've been offered a contract in Canada. They want me to design a new theatre on the west coast. It would be a sort of working honeymoon, but if you don't fancy that . . .'

'How often will I see you?' she asked doubtfully.

'All the time,' he murmured, trailing his lips across her cheeks. 'I'll drag you around with me when I have to inspect the site and you can lean over my shoulder while I draw up the plans, and then, of course, there'll be the nights . . .'

'We'll take it!' she said firmly, snuggling up to him, and after a while she said, 'It seems to me that my job is now finished, the bargain completed. So you owe me fifteen thousand pounds, Mr Forrest!'

'Agreed!' he assured her swiftly. 'Will you take it in cash or in kind?'

'What kind?' she asked suspiciously.

'This kind, darling,' he murmured softly, folding her tightly against him, his hands stroking her willing body as his lips covered hers. 'How long can I have to pay it off?' he asked thickly when she stirred from the enchantment.

'How long do you need?' Merissa asked winsomely, her fingers trailing through his thick hair as he leaned over her.

'For ever?' he asked softly. 'Continuous instalments?'

'I agree,' she whispered back, smiling into his eyes as he stood and lifted her into his arms.

'I'd better start now,' he said huskily. 'I owe you such a lot. It might just take longer than for ever.'

Step into a world of pulsing adventure, gripping emotion and lush sensuality with these evocative love stories penned by today's best-selling authors in the highest romantic tradition. Pursuing their passionate dreams against a backdrop of the past's most colorful and dramatic moments, our vibrant heroines and dashing heroes will make history come alive for you.

Watch for two new Harlequin Historicals each month, available wherever Harlequin books are sold. History was never so much fun—you won't want to miss a single moment!

Harlequin American Romance

Romances that go one step farther...
American Romance

Realistic stories involving people you can relate to and care about.

Compelling relationships between the mature men and women of today's world.

Romances that capture the core of genuine emotions between a man and a woman.

Join us each month for four new titles wherever paperback books are sold.
Enter the world of American Romance.

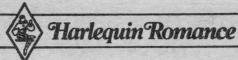

Harlequin Romance

ATTRACTIVE, SPACE SAVING BOOK RACK

Display your most prized novels on this handsome and sturdy book rack. The hand-rubbed walnut finish will blend into your library decor with quiet elegance, providing a practical organizer for your favorite hard-or soft-covered books.

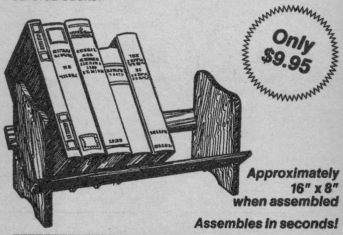

Only $9.95

Approximately 16" x 8" when assembled

Assembles in seconds!
